Kiwi in Cat City

by Vickie Johnstone

With illustrations by
Nikki McBroom

Kiwi in Cat City
Copyright April 2002, Vickie Johnstone
Published by Vickie Johnstone, April 28, 2011

Cover image: iStockphoto/minimal
Edited by Vickie Johnstone

Illustrated by Nikki McBroom:
www.tridentartanddesign.weebly.com

Edited by Susan Bennett, but revised since

Acknowledgements

This book was inspired by Kiwi, a very fluffy, cheeky little black cat I used to have. It is dedicated to cat lovers of all ages and anyone who ever imagined what it might be like to be a cat for one day. I hope you enjoy.

For readers aged 9 up

Kiwi and the Missing Magic (book 2)
Kiwi and the Living Nightmare (book 3)
Kiwi and the Serpent of the Isle (book 4)
Kiwi in the Realm of Ra (book 5)
Kiwi's Christmas Tail (book 6)

For readers aged 13 up

Day of the Living Pizza (book 1)
Day of the Pesky Shadow (book 2)
The Sea Inside

Prologue

She was as black as night that lost its moon
She was a crazy kind of loon.
Eyes as wide as giant saucers
Yellow and rimmed with green;
Whiskers long with almost white tips
She grinned an unmistakable feline grin.
Her walk was kind of majestic
Yet pretty funny at top speed
For hers was not a slimline figure,
Rather a bit on the curvy side,
And when she rolled on her back
Black soft fur fluffed up.
Little paws as soft as velvet
But beware the quick glint of claws
Curved and sharp as a knife.
She would squint at you and purr
The most wondrous hum
And you'd forget all your troubles
Rushed along on the ride of sound.
Her name was Kiwi
But she was no ordinary cat.
When the moon was full
Like a cat's claw
Her ears would prick up
Her whiskers twitched
Her tail stood up tall and bold
And she'd follow her nose
Out into the cool night air.
Until one eerie cold night
When everything changed…

Introduction

The night hung like a heavy, dark blanket through which the tiniest silver stars twinkled. Far below, the lamps shone a blue wash across the cobbled streets. Not a breeze blew and all was quiet. The little houses sat motionless with their curtains drawn and nearly everyone was tucked up in bed asleep. Mr Katz looked at his watch. He was running late. Dinner would be on the table and he was not there to eat it. His belly rumbled and his nose twitched, as it always did when he was hungry.

Mr Katz began to dream of food – lashings of mouthwatering goodies, mountains of them, and a nice, warm mug of milk to send him off to sleep. He smiled at the idea. If only he was tucked up in bed, nice and warm, with a steaming mug of…

Tap, tap, tap!

From somewhere behind Mr Katz drifted the sound of footsteps in the dead night. They started in the distance, but became louder. He turned to see who was out this late, but there was no one there. How strange, he thought. The footsteps sounded closer. Feeling nervous, he stopped whistling and quickened his pace.

Around the corner of the street went Mr Katz, walking fast, his breathing growing heavier. He could hear the echo of steps approaching, nearer and nearer. Turning, he looked again, but he couldn't see anyone in the darkness. He turned the next corner and the next. Still, the footsteps followed, louder and louder, nearer and nearer, faster and faster.

Tap, tap, tap!

Mr Katz broke into a run. He dropped his work bag and sped around the next corner, and the next, and the next. Bang! He stopped all of a sudden.

"Are you alright sir? You seem in a hurry tonight," said a female voice.

Mr Katz puffed and panted, feeling quite out of breath. He squinted, but could not see her face properly. "Yes, I'm alright," he answered. "I'm sorry. I didn't mean to scare you. I was in a bit of a rush."

"So it seems," she said, "but you ran in the wrong direction."

Mr Katz felt someone grab him from behind. "You really should have gone the other way," said a male voice.

Mr Katz shivered from the tips of his whiskers all the way down to the end of his tail.

Chapter 1: Follow, follow

Amy awoke to see her black cat sitting perched on the end of her bed, studying the gleaming moon outside. She rubbed her eyes and sat up just in time to see Kiwi leap out of the open window and on to the ledge below.

Amy crept out of bed, padded to the window in her bare feet and peered out. The cat was standing perfectly balanced on the wooden garden fence, calm and still, her tail perked up. For a while, Amy watched the dark silhouette staring up at the moon. I wonder where Kiwi will go tonight, she thought, and in that moment she had an idea. Creeping quietly into the bedroom of her brother, James, who was sleeping soundly, she prodded his arm until he woke with a jump.

"What?" he whined, wiping the sleep out of his eyes. "I was dreaming!"

"Come and look."

"Eh?" Stumbling out of bed, he followed his sister like a zombie to the window. Gazing out, he spotted the black cat sitting on the garden fence.

"She has been sitting there for ages," said Amy.

James shrugged. "Maybe she's stretching."

The children watched, but Kiwi didn't stretch. Instead she leapt off the fence and stood on the path, looking up at the moon.

"Now that's weird. That's what I'm talking about," said Amy. "She's thinking about something."

"I wonder where she goes at night," James mused.

Amy grinned. "Mouse hunting!"

"Yuck, she wouldn't, would she?"

"Tell you what, I'm going to follow her and see."

"You're crazy," gasped James. "It's the middle of the night. Mum will kill you."

"I want to see what she has for breakfast," Amy said, laughing. "Don't you?"

"Yuck! That's grim," said James, screwing up his face.

Amy wandered back to her bedroom with her little brother following, looking half asleep and half confused. "So you're coming then?" she asked, putting on her trainers and pulling her jacket over her nightdress.

"Erm," he murmured as his sister tiptoed out of the room. "Okay, but if Kiwi catches anything, I'm not touching it."

James put on his trainers, jeans and jacket, and crept down the stairs after his sister, being careful not to make a sound. He could hear his dad snoring like a sleeping dragon. The noise echoed off every wall. Brother and sister made it quietly to the back door, and opened it carefully on its old hinges. It creaked so loudly that the children feared their parents might wake.

Kiwi was still sitting in the middle of the garden, staring up at the moon. Holding their breath, the children closed the back door without a sound. Turning around, they were just in time to see the black cat plunge over the fence in a single bound. Amy and James glanced at one another, raised their eyebrows and ran to the bottom of the garden. Opening the gate, out they went, giggling. It was a

6

warm summer night without a breeze. In the field beyond the gate, trees soared up against the night sky, like jagged spectres. Without the shine of the moon it would have been too dark to see anything at all.

James trembled, but he had already decided he was not going to look scared, even if he was.

"There she goes," said Amy, pointing.

Bounding across the field towards the black tail bobbing above the grass in the distance, they chased and chased, but Kiwi ran and ran. They swerved between trees and the black cat just kept going, and after a while they started to puff and pant. "Kiwi!" they yelled.

Suddenly, the little cat's ears pricked up and she stopped. Caught unawares, she spun around, her yellow eyes wide and enquiring. "Are you two following me?" she asked.

The children stopped dead in their tracks. James sat down on the grass with a bump, his mouth wide open. Amy wanted to say something, but she couldn't speak.

"Well, are you?" asked Kiwi, standing up straight on her hind legs and resting one front paw on her hip. "It's a bit late to be out playing, you know?"

The cat gave her biggest, widest grin and flicked her tail. Then she calmly sat down and started to wash herself, knowing she had just given her two playmates the biggest shock of their lives. She carried on licking her paw, flicked out a claw, and waited for a reply. It was a long time coming.

The children were transfixed, rooted to the spot. Cold fingers of air travelled up their spines and made all of the hairs on their necks stand up on end. Amy gulped. Was she dreaming?

"What's wrong?" mewed Kiwi with a chuckle. "Cat got your tongue?"

"Aaaah!" Amy sat down with a thump.

"Yooou taaalk!" James stuttered.

"Well, what were you expecting? Sign language?" asked Kiwi matter-of-factly.

"But, we can understand you," mumbled Amy, pinching her arm. "Ouch!" It hurt, which meant she was not dreaming. Could this be real after all?

"I know several languages," explained Kiwi. "It comes in handy. So you WERE following me? Ha ha!"

"Sort of," James admitted. "We were wondering what you ate for breakfast."

"Like mice?"

James nodded.

Kiwi laughed. "I have more important things to do, and mice taste funny – not good. And mice have feelings too. They're very intelligent, you know. I have several good friends who are mice…"

Kiwi stopped talking for a moment as the two children sat open-mouthed in shock, blinking oddly. "Alright, enough of that," she continued, thinking it best to change the subject. "I was joking. I don't have any mouse friends! Well, you see the moon way up there? See how it's really bright and glowing?"

The kids nodded.

"See how it's shaped like a cat's claw?"

"I guess so," said James.

"Nights like these are not ordinary nights," said the cat, looking straight at the boy.

James trembled. "Why?" He wasn't sure if he wanted to know the answer. Was Kiwi going to eat them?

"Well, if you really want to know, James, why don't you follow me some more?"

It was a challenge! Kiwi was grinning from ear to ear now. Amy felt cold, even though the air was warm. She could only stare awkwardly, as though hypnotised, while her brother chatted to the cat… the cat… THE CAT! She felt dizzy.

After a few more minutes, Kiwi gazed back at the moon. It seemed even brighter. Standing up, she flashed her big, yellow eyes. "There is no more time to lose. I have to go now. Are you coming?"

James sprung to his feet. "I'm coming," he announced.

9

"No," Amy cried out as her brother took two steps towards the little black cat. "I'm scared. Don't follow. This is too weird!"

But James didn't listen and carried on walking. Amy pulled herself to her feet and looked behind her. The field was empty. It must be about 2am by now, if not later. Morning was fast approaching and her parents would be getting up in a few hours for work. What should she do? She couldn't let her brother go alone. What if he got lost?

"Wait!" Amy shouted, charging after James and her suddenly talking cat. Things were not how they were meant to be today.

Chapter 2: As easy as one, two, three

"Come on," urged Kiwi. "We're nearly there."

"Nearly where?" asked James, glancing around at the big, open and completely empty field. All around the edges, the tall trees loomed, stretching up like a giant, natural wall.

"Here."

"But there's nothing here," said James, feeling slightly impatient. Not only could his pet cat talk, but she was also clearly crazy.

The cat smiled. "There's more than the eye can see. Just follow what I do, and concentrate – it's easy." Sitting down, she gazed up at the moon with her big, yellow saucer eyes and said, "One, two, three, a flick of the tail, a purr, a leap, and away we go…"

Puff! She vanished. All that remained was a strange, glowing, purple mist.

"She disappeared!" cried Amy, turning around in a circle. "I can't see her. Can you?"

"Your turn," James said quietly.

"What? Are you crazy? She must be hiding in the grass somewhere."

"You go first, like she said."

Amy looked annoyed. "You can't be serious? You're not suggesting…?"

James nodded. "You are the oldest."

"No way!" she replied. "I haven't got a tail to flick and I'm pretty sure I can't purr."

"I think you're meant to imagine one."

"You're mad!" said Amy.

"Mmm, I'm going to try," James sighed, and he starting counting out loud, "One, two…"

"Okay, okay," cried Amy, clenching her fists at her sides. "But, straight after this we're going home."

And so, Amy flicked her imaginary tail, which was pretty long in her mind, purred and leapt up into the air – whether into nothing or something, she couldn't quite make it out. She had this amazing feeling of pure weightlessness, as if her body weighed nothing. It also felt smaller and she seemed to be floating. All around her, everything turned the most luminous purple.

"Wow, it worked," shouted James, bouncing up and down. And then he collapsed on the ground in giggles. "Cool!"

In the spot where his sister had jumped into the air, only a puff of purple mist remained. Now it's my turn, he thought, and turning around with a "One, two, three" and a flick of his imaginary tail, a purr and a leap, away he went – to who knows where. A feeling of sheer weightlessness gave him the impression that he was flying. It was wild! But where was he flying to?

"Ahem, the landing can sometimes be a little difficult until you get used to it," said Kiwi, washing her nose with her paw as Amy found herself collapsed in a heap on the grass. "You'll have to get used to being on four feet now!"

"Four?" Amy stuttered, bewildered.

"Sure, look down and see how many feet you have."

Amy glanced down and could not believe her eyes. "Eeeeeek!" Kiwi was right. Not one, not two, not three, but four feet were attached to her new body – but they were not feet, they were paws! Fluffy black and white paws! "Impossible!" she screeched, jumping backwards and tripping over, unable to balance. But, the biggest shock of all was yet to come. Sticking out behind her was a big, white fluffy tail, which wiggled like a worm.

"Oh no!" Amy gasped, and then fell over again as she tried to move around in a circle to check out the tail properly. "Ah," she cried out, but then a small laugh bubbled up inside her, spilling over until she couldn't stop. She rolled over on to her back with her legs in the air – all four of them – and found herself unable to stop giggling. "I have a tail! A tail!" she said and laughed some more.

Just at that moment, James fell through the sky and bounced on the grass with a little "ouch", except, of course, it wasn't quite James. Well, it was and it wasn't. James was now a little tabby kitten with a very pink nose. He wobbled on his newfound paws as he walked with his tail stuck up straight like a radar. "Where's Amy?" he asked, feeling slightly dazed.

"Don't you recognise her?" asked Kiwi, nodding towards the little black-and-white cat, who sat bright eyed and staring at him.

"No, really, where is my sister? Is she okay?"

"I can see this is going to take a while," said Kiwi, deciding to explain things. "Amy, meet James. James, meet Amy. No, you're not dreaming. Yes, you have a tail."

13

The boy-kitten frowned. "You're joking?"

"I'm afraid she's not," purred Amy in her feline voice.

"Ah!" meowed James and fell over at the sound. Where was his voice? He then recognised the flowery necklace that the black-and-white cat was wearing and he sighed, or rather mewed again. "It can't be true! It can't! Hey, what's that? I've got a tail!" He glanced down. "Wow, four paws – no way! This tail is really bushy…"

Amy started giggling and Kiwi raised an eyebrow. It was going to be a long night. Humans!

Chapter 3: Purple mist

"Now, if you've both finished chattering, I'm going to show you around a little city that I happen to know," Kiwi announced.

"Is it far?" asked James, who was having a few walking problems, stumbling on his four paws. Out of the corner of his eye, he kept spying his tail jiggling around. The word weird just didn't cover it.

"We'll be there in the blink of an eye," said the yellow-eyed, black cat.

"Cool," purred Amy.

Not that you would know it, of course, but trying to walk on four legs when you are used to walking on two is a little tricky, especially when your brain is telling you to walk upright – a bit like trying to dance with four left feet. So, as you can imagine, progress was pretty slow for a while.

"Are we there yet?" asked James, after he'd almost tripped over his tail for the eleventh time.

"Ten more minutes," replied Kiwi with a grin. She remembered how the children's parents had told them this every twenty minutes in the car and it had been quite funny. "Have you practised your meows and purrs?" she asked.

The kittens looked at one another with worried, fluffy expressions. Meowing AND purring? At different times or at the same time – were both even possible?

After half an hour's walk through the field, they reached the edge of the forest and after ten more minutes they found themselves in a clearing. All around, the trees stretched up, dead straight and kind of scary looking.

"How will we find our way back?" asked Amy. "Everywhere looks the same."

"Stick with me," said Kiwi. "But if you get lost, remember that tree over there – if you stare at it long enough with your cat eyes you will see it change colour to purple. Pass by it, walk thirty minutes in a straight line and you'll be home."

"Purple tree? She's mad," whispered James, as it was brown, like all the others.

"Shush!" hissed Amy, not noticing she was hissing – just like a cat.

Kiwi stopped walking.

"Where now?" asked Amy, sitting down. She felt a strange urge to wash behind her ears, but so far she had managed to resist, and her whiskers were detecting all sorts of unusual sensations that she had never noticed before.

Kiwi flounced over to a crop of bright bluebells in the centre of the clearing and walked around them.

"What's she doing?" James asked Amy.

"I don't know."

"It's weird."

"No weirder than you look right now," whispered Amy, scratching behind her ears. She yelped as her little claws pressed too hard. "She's walking around in a circle – once, twice, three times... oh, now she's disappeared!"

Sure enough, all that was left of Kiwi was a purple mist, just like before.

"Are we supposed to follow her?" asked James.

"I think we get to choose," said Amy.

James grinned. "Let's go."

So they did. Three times around the bluebells and they vanished. Puff!

"What took you so long?" asked Kiwi when the kittens appeared beside her. "Are you having a good time so far?"

Brother and sister nodded. "Although it's a bit confusing," James added. "No offence, but being a cat is weird."

"Not weird," corrected Kiwi, "just different. Not everyone is the same." She looked them up and down, and smiled warmly. "You'll get used to it. I'll teach you how to hunt mice later."

"Eeeeeek, no!" cried James.

"I'm vegetarian!" said Amy, screwing up her nose.

Kiwi laughed. "I'm only joking. Come on, we're nearly there and I'm running late. Follow me, and remember to start practising those meows and purrs. Don't let anyone think you're not a cat."

Meow, purr, cough, meeeekkk, puh, puh, pooh, cough, meow, purrrrrrr.

After a while they found themselves in a long, curving tunnel, but it wasn't made of earth. The floor, ceiling and walls were covered with little blue and white tiles – an intricate mosaic of tiny cats. There was no light in the distance, so the tunnel had to be a long one. Now and then the tiles blinked and the eyes of the mosaic cats glowed to light the way, as if knowing when a feline – or someone – walked past.

To the children's astonishment, Kiwi began to whistle a tune. They didn't know cats whistled in private – did you? As they went further, Amy and James found it easier and easier to walk, and to control the long tails flapping behind them. Kiwi was right – walking on four paws wasn't that hard after all, and once you worked out how to keep your tail in the air there were no more embarrassing trip-ups.

After a while the mosaic cats changed colour to purple and the group of friends came across a small, purple door with the image of a big cat in the centre. The material was neither wood nor metal, or anything the children had ever seen before.

"Who is there?" asked a very small voice.

"Kiwi."

A peephole opened in the face of the cat on the door and some white whiskers popped out. "And they are…?"

"Friends," said Kiwi. "Ames and Jimster."

Jimster? I guess that's me, James realised. It was a cool name and more cat-like. I mean what cat would be called James?

"They are rather odd names," said the voice.

Kiwi shrugged. "I know, but, as we all know, humans aren't very good at choosing names. I got lumbered with Kiwi!"

"That's true," said the small voice. "You were named after a fruit. Come on through."

The door suddenly vanished.

Chapter 4: Cat City

"Welcome to Cat City," said the big, fat white cat – the owner of the very small voice. "We hope you have a very enjoyable day. Here's a brochure to help new visitors find their way around."

"Thanks," purred Amy and James, taking the small, square folded leaflets, which opened out like origami and popped up in the shape of cats.

"What strange accents," the white cat remarked, curious. "Are you from foreign shores?"

"Yes, they are," said Kiwi. "They haven't quite mastered the language. Poor school, you know."

"Ah, poor things." The white cat nodded. "Well, there's always time and they're young. Don't forget to check in at the Cat Motel. Mrs Ebenry is back too, with her famous mouse delicacies, and the fair is coming next week, so you'll find lots to do."

"Thanks," purred Kiwi, waving a paw. "Follow me," she told Amy and James. "And, whatever you do, don't speak, just purr or something!"

The kittens looked at her and nodded quietly. Amy wondered what mouse delicacies were. She had no idea, but they made her shiver. They stepped around the big, white cat whose nose seemed way too big for his round, chubby face, and his beady little eyes followed their every move. As the area behind him came into view, Amy gasped, amazed. "Wow!" she exclaimed.

Cat City was spectacularly colourful and made the human world seem very grey. They were wandering down the main street, but the road was paved with the same blue and white mosaic as the tunnel – beautiful designs of cats and paws. They glinted in the sunshine, which was bright and kind of orangey rather than the yellow of home. It made the city glow and sparkle. Everything – all the houses, buildings, shops and streetlights – was shrunk down to cat size, even the cars.

Cars?! Amy peered at them. They actually looked completely different to the ones she was used to, but they did the same thing – drove the cats around town. Instead of four wheels there were four paws, made of some unrecognisable material, which ran really fast when the vehicle started up. Vroom! A driver sped off in his little cat car. They didn't have roofs and the cats' heads stuck out, which was quite funny. James wondered what they all did when it rained, but then imagined it never did. Wow, no rain, he thought. That would be cool.

All of the buildings had cat-size doors with small, round glass windows and blue handles shaped like paws. Amy noticed there were not any cat flaps at all. Each shop had a sign with a cat reference – Cat Tools, Meow Café, Purrfect Mouse Burgers, Kitty Parlour, Insurance in a Whisker, Meow Market and Paws for Thought were a few.

All of the cats seemed to know Kiwi because they flicked their tails her way as she waltzed by. They also gave polite nods to Ames and Jimster while seeming to stare a little too long. James noticed whiskers twitching, and he wondered if the cats of this town would ever suspect that he and his sister were not real kittens.

Amy had never seen so many cats in her life, of every shape, size and colour, and they wore clothes! Little booties, trousers, waistcoats, dresses and even hats, jewellery and feathers! Some cats didn't wear anything, so she guessed it was a question of decoration and not necessity that some wore clothes while others went naked. Not a choice you could make easily at home when you were walking down the street! And no-one was smoking – excellent, she thought, having never liked the smell.

"It's sooo big," said James, stating the obvious.

"Of course," smiled Kiwi. "This is home – here, with all the catizens. Well, my real home from home when I'm not living with you."

The kittens were surprised. Catizens?

"How often do you visit?" asked Amy.

"All of the time," said Kiwi with an odd smile. "It's hard to explain. All to do with what you consider time to be, and it's a little complex. When you think I'm going out hunting at night, I'm here, and I'm back in no time, as you know. So, I might be away for a few hours, yet I've been here in Cat City for weeks or months. However, I have to be careful because when I'm at home – here – I can age, but I can't age in the human world. In fact, when I'm in your world I can rejuvenate and get some time back – like getting my beauty sleep, only more so."

The kittens' eyes popped open wide.

"Yes, it's mind-blowing, I guess, and top secret. Loads of feline physics and complicated cat logarithms are involved, so let's just say that when

21

you think I've wandered off to have a quick catnap, I'm probably here."

At the mention of mathematics, James' eyes began to glaze over and his mind went blank. His mouth fell open in a big yawn.

"Okay, let's move on to something more interesting," the black cat sighed.

Chapter 5: Cat Crime

"I'm going to introduce you to a very special friend of mine and business partner," Kiwi announced as she led the way around a street corner.

"You work here?" asked Amy, gazing up… and up and up.

They were standing in front of the biggest building in Cat City. The top was lost in the clouds. It was a gigantic, grey structure, which stood out from the rest of the houses and buildings in the city just because it lacked any colour. It looked very intimidating. The front door was also grey, but the knocker was bright red and small – so small you could miss it if you didn't know it was there. It was shaped like a cat's eye.

Perhaps the building is grey because it is trying to look scary, thought James. Perhaps it didn't want any visitors at all. A big sign turned around slowly on the patch of grass in front of the building. It read Cat Crime and it was grey, as was the grass. "It's kind of cool," he said. "Is this the police station?"

"Police station and investigative agency – the only one in Cat City," answered Kiwi. "Everyone comes here with their problems and we sort them out. We're here today because my friend is in a spot of trouble."

Amy's eyes lit up, her whiskers flicking about. "Are we going to help?"

Kiwi nodded. "That's the idea."

The black cat pushed open the very small door.

Amy noticed that, unlike the front door of her parent's house, it didn't squeak or creak at all. Inside, a big hallway opened up and a spiral staircase wound its way upwards, disappearing into the distance. There were no doors at all in the hallway, only an elevator with a huge sign that read Cat Lift. Everything inside was the same grey as the outside.

"It's the rule here," said Kiwi. "Everything is grey, except the catizens."

They climbed the spiral staircase. James, being quite small, jumped up each one with a kind of bunny hop. Amy tried not to laugh and concentrated on keeping her tail from wrapping around the central pole. Kiwi walked up smoothly, of course. Very professionally, Amy thought. They came to level one of the building and stepped off the stairs. James looked down and his vertigo kicked in, and he felt glad they didn't have to go up any higher.

Kiwi pushed open a heavy door and they all walked through, watched by a big cat's eye that blinked in a ball floating up and down the hallway. "Don't worry, it's a camera," she explained.

The room inside was decorated with many photographs of cats in uniforms, a big fluffy rug, and rows of bookcases filled with books. A bright blue light hung from the ceiling. What looked like a water machine sat in the corner, but James noticed it dripped a white liquid. He decided it must be milk. Everything was still grey, but slightly different. The blue light seemed to make objects change shade, so although everything was grey, they seemed to go through a rainbow of colours.

"Kitty nice day to you," said a voice.

Behind a big desk sat a skinny, black cat with a very thin moustache that was twisted at the ends. On his jacket was a little cat-shaped badge bearing the name of Toby. He had a big, cheerful smile, but Amy's attention was fixed on his huge caterpillar-like moustache. Remembering her mum said it was rude to stare, she quickly glanced away.

"Can I help you?" he asked.

"Yes," said Kiwi, striding over. "I'm Kiwi. We're here to see Inspector Furrball. He's expecting us. Or he was expecting us a while ago, but we only just got here. Are you new? I haven't seen you before."

"Yes, I am," said Toby. "I started working here about a month ago. I transferred to Cat City from a small town. Police work there was a bit slow. You know what I mean? Hum, I cannot see you on Inspector Furrball's list of expected visitors. If you could wait, I'll buzz him and tell him you're here. Right, okay, yes, he says he can see you. Please take the lift and go to level three and turn right."

"Thanks," said Kiwi, "and have a kitty nice day."

She knew which way to go, having visited Cat Crime hundreds of times. But, where was her good friend Kip, who used to have Toby's job? He had worked here for years.

The lift was, well, you can guess, very grey, but the blue light inside made it gleam a variety of shades. The lift sped up to level three, and stopped with a big shake and a massive bang. The walls trembled. Amy and James collapsed on the floor, and looked up to see that Kiwi had pinned herself up against the wall.

"Embarrassingly, we haven't quite mastered lift technology yet, but you'll get used to it," said the black cat as the kittens staggered to their paws.

As they exited the lift, rather quickly in case it decided to rush off, Amy and James noticed the corridor was a faint red colour – but under a layer of grey, it seemed – as were the floor, ceiling and doors.

"You may notice a red tint to everything here," said Kiwi. "This is the very heart of the building. Remember how we got here. There is only one way. If anything bad happens, or someone who shouldn't finds out the route, we change the way you can get to this room."

The kittens listened silently, their tails bobbing in odd directions. Amy wanted to scratch, but stopped herself. They followed Kiwi to the right and then to the left, and left again, and finally right, walking until they came to a red door with a sign perched on it: Inspector Furrball. Kiwi knocked three times and entered.

Inside, the sound of peculiar mewing music flooded their ears and a short, chubby, ginger tomcat bellowed "Hello" from the corner of the room. From behind a pair of round glasses, balanced on the end of a big pink nose, two bright golden eyes beamed out. He wore a bright red waistcoat with a golden watch hung on the end of a golden chain. It glinted and ticked silently.

"So, who have we here?" asked Inspector Furrball, stroking his whiskers. Amy noticed a small mouse key ring on his desk and shivered. Surely it must be a fake?!

"These are two friends of mine – Ames and Jimster," said Kiwi, pushing the bewildered kittens forward. "It's their first visit to Cat City."

"He-hell-ooo," they stammered in unison.

"Funny accents," said the inspector, peering forwards at them. "Have they got passes?"

"Not yet. I was hoping you could help with that," replied Kiwi.

"It shouldn't be a problem," said Furrball, "if you can vouch for them." He peered even more closely at the two kittens, feeling something was amiss, but then he waved the idea out of his head.

"Well," said Kiwi with a cough, trying to distract the inspector, whom she knew was too intelligent to be fooled for long, "I got a message by robin today that you need my help."

"Yes, I do, but first things first – are you two little ones thirsty?"

"No, I'm okay," said Amy, wondering what Kiwi meant by 'a message by robin'. Did a robin really send a message to her? Did he carry it in his beak or could birds speak to cats here? And didn't cats eat birds? It was all very confusing.

"Yes!" cried James with his tongue dangling out, forgetting to purr.

Furrball looked at him in surprise. He tapped the buzzer on his desk with his paw and asked someone to bring refreshments. Kiwi sat down on a red cushion and wrapped her tail around her. James and Amy copied, having found two unbelievably comfortable cushions on the red carpet. The door opened and a tall, grey cat in a green dress walked in, pushing a small trolley with running cat feet

27

underneath it. "Milk, cream, rice pudding, mousie mousse, grass shakes, yogurt or an assortment of biscuits – all lactose-free, of course," she announced.

"We'll have the rice pudding," chose Kiwi, thinking it safely resembled the human version. She was positive the kittens were not ready for milkshakes that tasted of grass.

"It's very good," said Miss Kitty, handing round little red saucers. Amy stifled a giggle and took one.

"Thank you, Miss Kitty," said Furrball, his face turning a little red. She smiled and left the room, closing the door behind her.

The inspector set a saucer on his desk, filled it with milk and quickly lapped it up, purring intermittently. The kittens stared in surprise. He didn't make any mess at all. Kiwi did the same and lapped it all up with a big purr. Oh no, thought Amy, there appeared to be no other way of drinking it and she was actually very thirsty. She glanced at James, who looked as confused as she felt. They nodded at one another, deciding to just go for it. So, they stuck their heads in their saucers and started licking the milk – and decorated the carpet, themselves and Kiwi's tail with splatters of thick double cream.

Furrball stared at them with an odd glint in his eye.

Kiwi froze. "Ah, kittens... what can you do?"

Silence cut the air for a few very long seconds.

"What can I say," replied Furrball at last, suddenly exploding into laughter. "I suppose we've all done it, and I guess they've had a tiring day."

Kiwi stuttered, not knowing how to reply. The

28

two kittens looked up sheepishly with white blobs of cream dripping off their whiskers and noses.

Amy wondered how she was going to wipe it off discreetly. With a sinking feeling, she realised it could mean having to spit on her paw and wash, like Kiwi did. Eeek, never, she thought. Reaching for the nearest napkin, she dabbed her mouth, but it was hard to grip with a paw and it kept dropping.

Furrball raised an eyebrow and looked directly at his friend. "Is there something you want to tell me, Kiwi?"

She paused, thinking how to get out of this one. "What has been happening in Cat City?" she enquired, changing the subject.

"You've been away rather long this time," said the inspector, sitting down and playing with his pen. This involved batting it around his desk loudly with his paw, but the kittens pretended not to notice. They still had cream-covered whiskers to deal with.

"The problem is catizens are going missing – about five so far. This is worrying for us and the mayor."

"Missing?" asked Kiwi surprised.

"Gone, vanished, puff, we don't know where. All five cases happened over the past five weeks – one a week. No trace. No clues. It's a mystery and really bothersome. As you know, this kind of thing doesn't usually happen here."

"It is strange," said Kiwi, mystified. "Have you interviewed anyone?"

"We made a start, but we haven't got anywhere so far. No one has seen or heard anything. We're at a dead end. All of the disappearances happened when the catizens were on their way home from work when it was dark. The last one was a Mr Katz."

"Mmm, I'll see if I can help," said Kiwi, concerned.

Furrball smiled. "I was hoping you'd say that. But there is one other thing…"

The kittens froze. This was it. He knew. They were about to be kicked out of Cat City for being fakers.

Furrball stopped smiling. "One of the five catizens who disappeared is Kip. In fact, he was the first. Five weeks ago."

"Oh no!" gasped Kiwi. "I was wondering where he was. I hope he's okay. We have to find him! I mean… them."

"I can let you have one of my Cat Squad to help you. If you need more, let me know, but please keep things quiet. We don't want to scare our catizens or alert whoever is doing this."

"And we want to get the catnapped home safe and sound," said Kiwi. "But, I don't think I need any help."

"Don't be kitty silly. It isn't a problem," said Furrball, waving his paw. "The Cat Squad is at your disposal. We have been testing some impressive new guns. Erm, that's probably not a good subject to talk about right now in front of the young ones. Sorry. Have you checked in at the Cat Motel?"

"Haven't had time," said Kiwi, looking troubled.

"I'll ring them and book your usual room plus two extra cushion baskets in it. Do you want a scratching post?"

"Great."

Suddenly there was a knock at the door. "Ah," said Furrball. "Here's the special agent. He's all yours. I think you've worked with him before."

On cue, a furry, brown face poked itself around the corner of the door.

"Paws?!" exclaimed Kiwi. "Oh no," she added, under her breath, "not him."

"Now, I must get on," said Furrball, smiling again. "Have a kitty nice day. Paws will be your right-hand tom."

Kiwi groaned. That's what I was afraid of, she thought, but she didn't say it out loud, because that would have been extremely rude.

Chapter 6: The alleyway

C at City was in darkness, lit by the faint blue glow of the streetlights, all of which had small, cat-shaped bulbs. Cats' eyes dotted the centre of every wide road, all the way up and down, providing light for the drivers, but there were no cat cars buzzing around tonight or any young felines out on their cat-boards. Instead, most of the catizens were at home. The streets had become much lonelier after dark since the disappearances began. Even the milk pubs were closed.

Four pairs of eyes peered around, belonging to four cats dressed in black, so they could hide in the shadows. They all wore balaclavas and little black boots, and they were very quiet. Their tails swept silently as they sat, waiting for something suspicious to happen.

"Five catizens have gone missing," whispered Kiwi. "One a week for the past five weeks, always on a Monday, so we can presume there will be one tonight, if we're lucky."

Lucky? I can think of luckier things, thought Amy.

"One what?" asked Paws, screwing up his eyes.

"A disappearance," said Kiwi, shushing him.

He frowned. "Why tonight?"

"Because it's the sixth-consecutive Monday."

"What's conservative?"

James giggled. Amy nudged him.

"Not conservative – consecutive. Tonight is the sixth week and the sixth Monday, and all of the other catizens vanished on a Monday," Kiwi explained.

Paws nodded. After a split second he frowned again. "I don't get it."

James and Amy looked at each other with raised cat eyebrows.

"One, two, three, four, five Mondays in a ROW," shouted Kiwi. "This is number SIX."

Bang!!!!! All of the cats sat up straight.

"W-what was t-that?" stammered Amy.

Paws shuddered and stepped quickly behind Amy. James hid behind Paws.

"The noise came from over there," said Kiwi, pointing. "I don't think the Cat Squad has checked out that area yet."

"They haven't?" asked Paws. "Maybe we should call them."

"No need. We can handle this. I thought you were my right-hand tom?"

"I am," said Paws, puffing out his chest. "I was just checking something back there."

Probably looking for his brain, thought Amy.

And his courage, thought James with a sigh. His hamster at home was braver and probably a whole lot smarter.

The alley was long and winding, leading off towards the eastern outskirts of the city. Its tall, brick walls created a narrow pathway that was pitch black and foreboding. Dustbins and rubbish littered both sides, and the cats had to be careful not to trip or knock anything over. The silence made it eerier. They could hear nothing except their own breathing and it was getting colder by the minute.

A spooky, claw-shaped moon hung in the sky above. Amy whispered to James that it was the same shape as the moon they had seen in their garden at home. It seemed so long ago.

The rooftops of adjoining houses towered way above and the children felt oddly small, but they now had an advantage: thanks to their cat-like forms and night vision, they could see in the dark as clearly as during the day. Their whiskers picked up some unusual vibrations too, and their sense of smell was stronger, although this was not a great benefit when they passed a pile of rotting fish that someone had forgotten to put inside a dustbin. "Eewww," mumbled James.

After saying how cool night vision was to one another a hundred times, the kittens felt less scared and began competing as to how far they could actually see. Finally, they settled down to the business of being investigators. The alley suddenly came to a fork, offering three directions. Which to choose?

"Why don't we split up?" suggested Paws.

"No, I don't think that's a wise idea," said Kiwi.

"Everyone knows that when the good guys split up, the monster gets them," said James. He knew what he was talking about. He'd seen this on TV. "They wander off and then the monster gets them one by one, because they don't have backup."

Paws sighed nervously while Amy laughed cat-style in a half purr, half splutter. Kiwi removed a tiny stick of chalk from the little pocket in her purple collar and marked the brick wall with an arrow. "This purple arrow will show us the way back. And you're right, Jimster, we're not going to split up under ANY circumstances. Agreed?"

Everyone agreed – they didn't need to think twice.

"Okay, follow me!" Kiwi chose the right fork and the other cats followed. Paws brought up the rear, his tail drooping. They walked about a hundred yards until they came to a high, wooden fence, which stretched upwards, surrounded by rooftops. A dead end.

"Let's go back," suggested Paws.

The cats turned around to do just that when a screeching meow pierced the night. They froze.

"Did you hear that?" asked Paws.

"No, I'm deaf," said James.

Paws pulled a face.

Kiwi glanced up at the fence and started pushing some dustbins together.

"Oh no," whispered Amy to James. "Is she going to do what I think?"

James nodded. "Yep."

Amy sighed. "I'm rubbish at the high jump."

"Alright," said Paws, rubbing his paws together excitedly.

"But, I–" James hesitated.

"Just jump," whispered Kiwi. "Trust me. Remember the 'one, two, three' in the field? It's as easy as that."

"Me first," said Paws, disappearing over the top.

"Okay, wait here," Kiwi told the kittens. She leapt on to the tall fence and vanished somewhere over the other side. A few minutes later, she reappeared on top of the wood. "Come on. It's quiet."

"Over there?" gulped Amy.

"Do we have to?" asked James. The idea was really spooky.

Kiwi shrugged. "No, you can stay here if you want."

Quivering slightly, Amy and James looked around. Staying where they were appeared to be equally spooky.

"Okay, wait up, Kiwi," Amy whispered. "We just need to work out how to get up there."

One jump on to the dustbin followed by one on to the fence should do it, she thought. Amy took a little leap and was surprised how nimble she was. She sailed through the air smoothly, hit the bin and sailed off again on to the top of the fence with a flick of her tail. Magic! Amy smiled. If only she could jump this well all the time. She would win the high jump at school and be the champion at hurdles.

Then it was James' turn. He took a deep breath, closed his eyes and leapt, hoping he would not fall and look stupid compared to his sister. But he need not have feared. Two smooth jumps later, he found himself on the fence, grinning from ear to ear. He hadn't wobbled one bit – he had perfect balance. Now that was something he never had before.

"Can we do it again?" pleaded the kittens in unison.

"I thought you might say that," said Kiwi, "but there's no time, I'm afraid. We must hurry. That bungling idiot, Paws, has wandered off to do some heroics. I was scared that might happen. Straight out of Cat Squad School and Furrball expects me to show him the ropes. How can I when he won't listen to anything? Now we have to find him as well. Come on."

Kiwi, with the two kittens following close behind, inched her way along the fence and the gutter. It was a long way down and James' fear of heights made him wobble, but the feeling seemed to be fading somehow. Maybe cats just didn't get vertigo?

The roof was very steep with some tiles missing, but the group managed to balance their way along it. The place was quiet, perhaps too quiet, and it was very, very dark indeed. In the distant sky, the claw-shaped moon gleamed brightly.

Out of the blue there was a high-pitched meow. Kiwi stopped suddenly and the kittens banged into her like dominoes. The meow was very close and coming from below them. Right below in fact, from inside the building on which they were standing. The kittens sniffed the air.

"Follow me," said Kiwi, bounding across the rooftop and the kittens did so, moving swiftly and easily. Soon they reached a small, spotlight window. Being as quiet as possible, they peered into the room beyond. A light was on, but they couldn't see anyone inside.

"Do you really think it's a good idea to go in?" asked James. "Remember, I'm only nine."

"That's almost leaving kittenhood in cat years," replied Kiwi. "Besides, I'll always look out for you."

Chapter 7: Across the rooftops

The three friends peered into the shaft of blue light below them, which made their faces light up. The low sound of voices travelled upwards and Kiwi nodded. Three sets of four paws tiptoed soundlessly across the roof and three mouths held their breath. Kiwi's collar tried not to jingle. At the very end of the roof there was a small, cat-shaped flap.

"Shush," whispered Kiwi. "Now you need to concentrate or I'll have to go alone."

"We're concentrating," said James.

"Mum will ground us if anything happens to you," Amy added.

"Then here goes," said Kiwi. "Easy does it."

Without further ado, the black cat pushed her head against the cat flap and disappeared into the sloping roof, her tail forming a question mark as the darkness swallowed it up.

James made a small gulp. "This is kind of scary."

"Sure is," agreed Amy.

"But exciting," he added.

She smiled. "Agreed!"

"Are we going in?"

"If we don't, do you know how to get home?" Amy asked.

"No."

"Then I guess we're going in."

Within two seconds, the two kittens had leapt through the cat flap. Inside, a single blue cat-shaped bulb swung from the ceiling of what appeared to be a very long corridor that turned at the end.

"Spooky," said James and Amy blinked. She could just make out the tip of a black tail disappearing around the end of the corridor. "Look, there's Kiwi! She must have thought we'd chicken out."

The two kittens scampered down the creaky floorboards and skidded around the somewhat tight corner, before scampering on again. "Wait for us!" James called out.

Kiwi flicked her tail and turned two bright eyes on the little scamps. "Concentrate!" she said.

The two kittens stopped and nodded. Then all three tiptoed down the corridor, around the next corner, and tiptoed some more. They passed several locked doors. The place was an endless, blue-lit maze. After what seemed an eternity they reached a massive door, marked 'Private'.

"Aha," said Kiwi, raising a crafty eyebrow. "Now we're getting somewhere."

With a big surge of effort and a unanimous heave, the three cats pushed the door... and plunged headfirst through it.

"What the kitty?" mewed Kiwi.

"I'm moving!" gasped Amy. "Ooooeeeeweee!"

"Ahh, I can't see!" squeaked James. "Ooww!"

They were speeding through the air at a tremendous pace, going downwards, faster and faster, further and further, quicker and quicker, until there sounded an enormous thud as they all stopped suddenly with a bump... outside!

"What was that?" moaned James.

"Where are we?" asked Amy. "Ouch, my head hurts."

Kiwi sighed. "We appear to have taken a trip down someone's very special slide. We have been ejected."

Amy rubbed her head. "Why?"

"I don't know, but I'm going to find out. Someone doesn't want visitors. There must be another way in."

"Or another way out," suggested Amy, washing the dirt off her face with her paw. Realising what she was doing, she stopped immediately. Yuck! My own spit! Yikes!

"What are we going to do now?" asked James.

"Hey!" called a voice in the darkness. "I've been hunting you everywhere. Where in Cat City did you get to?"

It was Paws, grinning from ear to ear. "You all look a little dirty. I checked around the whole building and didn't see anything suspicious. That is until I saw you three camping out here." He chuckled before striding off down the alley with his tail in the air.

"Ha ha, very funny," shouted Kiwi, jumping to her paws. "Okay, you two, what do you say to heading back to the Cat Motel for some milk and cookies?"

"Yeah!" purred Amy and James.

"I think we've had enough adventure for one night," said Kiwi. "I'm sure tomorrow will bring more surprises."

"Tomorrow?" asked James, yawning. "Shouldn't we be going home?"

40

Kiwi flashed her yellow eyes and grinned. "In your world you've only been gone for the shortest time. Think of one day here as one minute there."

Speechless, the kittens stared at Kiwi in shock.

"Cat loggies," remembered James. "I mean logs. Erm?"

"Logarithms," Kiwi corrected as she led them on their way.

Chapter 8: Back at Cat Crime

"I'm guessing you didn't find anything last night," said Inspector Furrball, leaning back in his chair to scrutinise the *Morning Meow*, "because we seem to have another missing catizen – it's even in the newspaper! Look – the headline says 'More Monday Mayhem'."

"Another?" cried James.

Kiwi didn't look surprised. "It stands to reason – consecutive Mondays."

"So someone hates Mondays, just like Dad," joked James. Amy nudged him with her tail.

Kiwi continued, "We're looking at serial catnappings, but why would anyone want to catnap so many catizens?"

The stout ginger tom threw the newspaper down on his desk and paced the room with his tail twitching. The clock on the wall ticked loudly, its tail-shaped hands counting down the minutes.

"My old friend, I do think something odd is going on."

"You don't say, Kiwi?" said Furrball. "Another victim and my Cat Squad is no nearer to finding out who is doing this or why."

"I hate to say it, but I think there will be more."

"Things are not looking good. That's six now. The mayor is nervous, the city is nervous, and I'm very nervous," said Furrball. "The mayor wants to bring in a curfew every night before the streets get dark."

"But Cat City hasn't had a curfew for years," gasped Kiwi, astonished. "It will make the catizens scared to go out at all."

Furrball stopped pacing. "Perhaps it will be a good thing and keep everyone safer. All of the catnappings have happened at night, and my department has to be seen to be doing something or the catizens will lose faith in us."

Kiwi scanned the *Morning Meow* and placed it back on the desk. Amy and James leaned across to take a look, but the writing was unreadable, like scribbled hieroglyphics. It was in cat-tongue. They looked at one another and at Kiwi, who twitched a whisker. Oops, thought Amy. The kittens then pretended to read the article, giving each other knowing nods, hums and the odd "Ah", so as not to arouse suspicion.

"Very interesting," said Amy.

"Yes. Very, very interesting," said James.

"Very strange."

"Yes. Very, very strange."

"I was particularly concerned about the part where…"

"Yes, well, Furrball," cried Kiwi, jumping up. "If you think you should introduce a curfew, do it. At least it will keep the catizens at home at night, like you said. Perhaps you should put more Cat Squaddies on the streets to make them feel safe too. Have you no leads at all?"

"No," said Furrball. "We are doing door-to-door interviews and searches, but we've come up with nothing. Normally a catnapper would make a demand for a ransom."

"Unless," said Kiwi, scratching her nose, "they have no demands to make."

"That would be most unusual. If money is not the motive, what is?"

"Perhaps they don't intend to return the six catizens," suggested Kiwi.

The inspector sat down. "You might have a point there," he said, chewing on something that vaguely resembled a mouse tail.

Amy and James pretended not to look while trying even harder not to feel ill. "Hope we never have to do that," whispered Amy.

"He's purring," said James. "It must taste good."

Amy felt queasy. "Maybe we should try to get fake ones, so we can just pretend."

Kiwi meowed and the kittens stopped talking. "There was one thing I was wondering about," she said.

"Yes?" asked the inspector, his eyes widening and hoping his friend had an idea. She often had fine ideas.

"There's a building at the far eastern side of the city. We found it when we explored the other night. We heard a meow, so we went inside the building. Some kind of warehouse, I think."

"Show me on the map where it is," said Furrball. Striding over to the wall, he pulled a cord that hung from the ceiling and down rolled a brightly coloured map. Cat City, a sprawling, intricate maze of streets, stretched out in all its glory.

James rushed over for a closer look. "Wow, the city is that huge?"

"Yes, it dates back thousands of years," said

Furrball, stroking his whiskers. "Where exactly is that alley you were talking about?"

Kiwi pointed.

Furrball peered closely. "Ah, I see, it's on the outskirts. That's an old part of the city. I'll just check the *Cat Business Log* for the address of that building. It looks big – probably a factory."

He pulled a huge, red book from the bookshelf and flicked to the index, which was in the middle for some reason, and soon found the page he was looking for. "Aha, the property is at numbers 12-54 Scratchington Lane. That is one of the original parts of the city, kittens, and it is a very old building. Ah, yes, I thought the name rang a bell. The owner is a Mr J Catskins and the company is Catskins Limited. They make biscuits – the Catskins brand, which is kitty nice. Yes, Mr J Catskins bought the building a year ago from Madame Purrfect. I do remember her."

A dazed look passed over Furrball's face and he closed the book. "Nice lady cat," he said. "She took early retirement from the biscuit business, sold the factory and went on a cruise. It turned into a long cruise. I'm not sure where she is now." He gazed out of the window to a point far off in the distance.

Amy sighed as the ginger tom had a dreamy look on his face. James looked bored and bent down to lick his tail. When he realised what he was doing, he coughed out some fur. Amy's eyes widened.

"So Mr J Catskins makes biscuits for Cat City only?" asked Kiwi, bringing the inspector back to the point.

"Not only," said Furrball. "His factory makes them and they are exported beyond Cat City, as well as being sold here. He really does make the best biscuits in town. He imports the ingredients, makes the biscuits and exports them. Wish I knew how to make them myself."

Suddenly there was a loud knock at the door. "Come in," he called out.

The door opened. "Paws, sir, reporting for duty," announced the brown cat.

"I guess we had better be going," said Kiwi. "You have a lot to do."

"Yes," said Furrball with a sigh. "We've a lot more training to do, haven't we, Paws?"

Amy and James smirked at each other. Once outside the office, Kiwi turned to them and said, "Sorry about the rush, but I thought we better leave quickly before Paws was assigned to us again!"

Amy laughed. "He is a bit on the dopey side."

James giggled, which, incidentally, came out as a squeaky purr that took him by surprise.

"What do we do now?" asked Amy. "We didn't tell the inspector about the slide thing…"

"Next time," said Kiwi. "Now it's time for some refreshments and then we investigate."

"But we've got nothing to go on."

"Yes, we do. I think we should investigate Catskins," Kiwi replied with a wink. "I have a hunch and you should always follow your instincts."

I never knew cats could wink.

Chapter 9: At the gate

"Well, hello again, you wee rascals!" smiled the big, white catizen with the very small voice at the gate to Cat City. "How are you enjoying your stay?"

"It's cool," said James.

Amy nodded. "We've seen loads and met…"

"Yes, well," purred Kiwi, curling her tail, "I have a couple of questions I've been meaning to ask you." She flashed her bright yellow eyes.

"Ah," squeaked the white cat, dropping his pen and perking up his ears, the tips of which had gone very pink. "Anything for you, Kiwi."

Amy and James gawped at him in bewilderment.

"Well," Kiwi purred, "I'm on police business, and I'd like to know exactly who has passed in and out of Cat City during the past month." She flicked her ear with her paw.

"That's easy," said the fluffy white cat. "And please call me Georgy."

Amy and James silently crept away in fits of giggly purrs.

Georgy heaved something heavy from down by his paws. "I log everything in this green book. I write everyone's name and company, and his or her reason for entering or leaving the city."

"Does anyone else have a copy?" Kiwi asked.

"Inspector Furrball gets to read a copy every week, but the book stays in the safe under there," said Georgy, pointing. "It's very strong and secure."

"I see. Can I take a look at the book?"

The white cat beamed. "Yes, certainly. I trust you.

Take all the time you need. Maybe I could take you out for a bowl of milk or something?"

Kiwi smiled. "I'm quite busy at the moment with this case, but maybe some other time."

"Or would you like some of my cream? It's thick, double cream. I bought it fresh today."

"No, I'm fine," said Kiwi.

"Or some cat biscuits? I have Catskins."

"No, really," she said, checking the book.

"Or I could run down to Mrs Ebenry's for some of her famous mouse delicacies?"

"No, I'm honestly fine."

"Alright, but please call me Georgy." The white cat smiled, showing perfect teeth and some sharp incisors, and placed his paw on top of Kiwi's.

She looked up, feeling slightly irritated. "I suppose one mouse delicacy would be good, but only the one. I'll watch the gate while you are gone."

He looked about to explode with delight. "And would you two little kitties like some of our famous mouse delicacies?"

"No!" they meowed loudly.

"Oh," said Georgy, slightly taken aback.

"They've just eaten," Kiwi explained.

He nodded, fidgeted for a moment and then scampered off towards Mrs Ebenry's famous shop, full of sugary concoctions.

"Eeew, I hope I never have to eat any," wailed Amy.

"You don't know what you're missing! Okay, this is what I was looking for," Kiwi said, running her paw down the page. "As you can see, there are many companies listed, and here is Catskins."

"And there's us…" pointed James.

"Yesssss," said Kiwi, "but there's Catskins."

"Is that good?" asked Amy.

Kiwi sighed. "Yes and no. There have been three deliveries per week during the past month, but only one delivery went out. That was more than six weeks ago, before the catnappings began. I was hoping to see more going out. Oh well." She closed the book and twitched her nose.

"Aha, good, you're still here! I'm just in time," squeaked a very small voice. A white paw held out a lavender box, tied with a purple ribbon and sprinkled with some shiny, purple glitter. Amy and James screwed up their noses, and backed away.

"Why, thank you very much," said Kiwi, who beamed and waved goodbye to Georgy. "We must go now. Very late, you know."

Georgy continued to stare as the black cat and the two kittens wandered off into the distance. He smiled and sighed. That Kiwi was one ladycat in a million.

"Where next, Kiwi?" asked Amy, flicking her tail to chase away a rather bothersome fly.

"I think it's back to Cat Crime for us, to find out who these missing catizens are."

Chapter 10: Cat Crime and Georgy

nspector Furrball showed Kiwi, Amy and James down to the second floor, which was full of busy catizens, all wearing red waistcoats and cat-shaped, gold badges stamped with 'Cat Squad' and their own name. The squaddies scurried back and forth between filing cabinets, charts and computers.

"This is the investigation room where everything happens," explained Kiwi.

"Wow," remarked James. "Impressive. How many people – I mean catizens – work here?"

"About two hundred in the building," said Furrball, leading them between the rows of desks to a filing cabinet at the far end of the room. He removed six red files. "Here you are," he said, handing them to Kiwi. "These are the files of the missing catizens. If you need more information, ask Detective Siam – he's the Siamese sitting in the corner over there. He's our new computer whiz. You might find his accent a little difficult to understand at first, but he'll track down anything. I have to go back upstairs now to go through some more training with Paws, and I have to arrange another meeting with Mayor Tom!"

"Thanks," said Kiwi.

Furrball was about to leave when he seemed to remember something. Digging his right paw into his waistcoat pocket, he pulled out two purple collars, which he placed on the table. "Before I forget, these are the passes I promised for the two kittens. There are emergency alarms on the inside, just in case."

"Thank you," said Kiwi. "That's kitty nice of you."

Furrball headed off and the kittens gathered around the table. Kiwi picked up the red folders and laid them out in a row. Each one was stamped with 'Cat Crime' in gold lettering, but the rest of the words were hazy.

"It says 'Missing Catizens'," translated Kiwi, noticing the kittens' confused expressions. She opened the folders. Inside each one was a picture of the missing catizen, along with some details about them and where they were last seen. Looking sad, Kiwi paused for a moment on the picture of Kip before flipping through the others. "Try to memorise their faces," she said. "It might come in handy."

The kittens studied the mug shots while Kiwi read out the notes. "It seems the missing catizens didn't know each other. They are not related, they went missing from different places and they did not work together. Basically, they have nothing in common. No wonder Furrball is flummoxed. None of them has a crimicat record either."

"So, nothing to go on," James commented.

"Not a whisker," said Kiwi, frowning. "A builder, a carpenter, a plasterer, a plumber, an electrician and a police cat."

"What if we check them on the computer?" asked Amy.

Kiwi shrugged. "It's worth a try." She wandered over to the Siamese cat. He looked quite young and intelligent in a mad scientist kind of way. A thinly-framed pair of round spectacles sat on his nose. His whiskers were bent in odd directions and his fur was a little wild. Amy thought he looked in need of a good meal, but she instinctively liked him.

"How can I help?" asked Siam, removing his spectacles and turning away from the stream of cat-mail messages on his computer screen.

Kiwi passed him the red folders. "Can you read these, please, and cross-check all of the information to see if there are any links?"

"Nothing is too difficult for Siam," he replied, smiling. "Do you want to wait around for the results?"

"No, we have a lot to do. Just buzz me on my catpad. My number is 558-6."

"Okey dokey."

Kiwi led the kittens a short distance away, stopped and held up one of her front paws. It was inlaid with a blue, shiny cat's head. "It's like one of your mobile phones and I speak into it," she explained. "I can remove it too!"

"Wow!" said James. "Very James Bond!"

"Can I have one?" asked Amy.

Kiwi laughed. "I don't think your parents would be impressed to see a microchip embedded in your hand!"

"I guess not," sighed James. His friends at school would have been so jealous.

"What's next?" asked Amy.

Kiwi thought. "I think we should check the deliveries at the Catskins factory, as something smells fishy there, but I have a little shopping to do first."

"Shopping?" asked Amy, thinking it odd timing.

***

Back at the gates to Cat City, Georgy spotted three figures sauntering down the street and he started waving his paw excitedly. Kiwi was returning and that made his day. "Hello, hello!" he called out, bouncing up and down, before they had even spotted him. "Hello, Miss Kiwi. How are you this kitty fine day?"

Kiwi forced a smile. "I'm still fine," she purred. "I wonder if you could do me another big favour? In exchange I have a present for you, from Mrs Ebenry!"

Georgy's eyes lit up as he took the small, lavender box, neatly gift-wrapped with a bow and covered in some tinsel that sparkled in the sun.

"Can you buzz me on my catpad when you get a delivery to, or from, the Catskins factory? It is top secret. I don't need to add that Inspector Furrball and I, of course, will be very grateful for your help."

The white catizen beamed. "Kitt-e-o."

"In the meantime," said Kiwi, turning to the kittens, "we can have a nice catnap in the sun."

The kittens agreed it sounded a very good idea.

***

A few hours and a buzz on the catpad later, the three friends trotted back to the gate to chat with Georgy, who wheeled out a crate stamped with 'Catskins Special Delivery'. Kiwi prised the lid off with her claw. They all looked in the box, except for Georgy, whom Kiwi asked to leave for a short while – police work and all that. Inside there were some neatly stacked packets of biscuits. Nothing strange about that.

Kiwi emptied the crate and discovered nothing suspicious at all. "Oh well," she said, disappointed. "I guess that would have been far too easy."

Amy wondered if the biscuits were tasty. Would they be made of mice or dead rats, or pigeons? Eeh!

"Are we going to stop investigating them now?" asked James.

"Not necessarily," said Kiwi. "I have a hunch and…"

"You should always follow your instincts," finished Amy.

The black cat smiled. "Indeed. You're learning fast."

"Why is that?" asked James.

"Because you never know when you might be exactly right. Come on, kittens – we've got a mystery to solve."

Chapter 11: Up the chute

"What's your plan?" asked Amy.

"I think we'll start by going over the same ground as last night and see where that takes us," said Kiwi.

James gulped. "Back to the alleyway? Isn't that dangerous?"

"We haven't got that bungling idiot, Paws, with us, so that should help us a lot," said Kiwi. "If we run into any trouble, I can give the inspector a buzz on my catpad."

The kittens looked at each other and shrugged. Amy decided to pretend she was a heroine such as Catwoman and James imagined he was James Bond. Yeah, Bond would never be scared of anything, he thought.

An hour later, the three cats were back at the scene of the previous night's shenanigans.

"Yesterday, Amy suggested there might be another way out," said Kiwi. "That got me thinking. Let's check the spot where we came out."

"How will we find it in the dark?" asked James.

"We can use another sense that is stronger in cats – smell!" said Kiwi, wiggling her nose. "As cats, you may have noticed your sense of smell has improved quite a lot."

This was true. Amy had noticed her brother was much smellier than normal and not because he had forgotten to change his socks for a couple of days. Cats don't wear socks anyway. He had to take them off, even when he got cold, because he just looked too weird. Have you ever seen a cat wearing socks? Nope, neither have I.

The kittens followed as Kiwi pursued an invisible trail of scent from the alleyway, around the side of the building, behind some trees and up to a small cat flap at the bottom of a high, stone wall. "Here we are," she said. "This appears to be the exit from our speedy little ride. What do you two budding detectives think we should do next?"

"Have a look inside," suggested Amy shyly.

"Run away!" James joked.

Kiwi laughed and pushed at the cat flap with her nose. When it didn't move inwards, she hooked a claw underneath the bottom of the metal and pulled it out, and then wriggled her head underneath and into the gap beyond. A rush of cold air blew back her ears and whiskers. The two kittens crawled under her arched belly. Inside, they spotted a long, smooth chute winding its way upwards as far as the eye could see. The gap between the two edges of the chute was about the same width as a cat's body.

The two kittens looked at Kiwi. On her face was a big smile. In that split second they knew what she was thinking and their eyes widened.

"Okay guys, we're going up!" she announced.

"What?" Amy cried.

"How?" squeaked James, staring up the slippery looking chute, the top of which disappeared into darkness. He gulped.

"Where's your sense of adventure?" asked Kiwi. "You just need to hold on to my tail."

"You're crazy," said Amy.

"Yes, well, it has been mentioned…"

"What if we accidentally let go?" cried James.

"You'll get a nice, long slide all the way down, which won't hurt at all."

Kiwi prepared herself for the climb by doing some cat yoga; pointing her bottom in the air, stretching her paws, craning her neck. Yes, she was soon fully prepared for action. She laid herself across the width of the chute and hooked her paws on either side, her claws providing a strong grip, with her belly suspended in the middle. "Now, you two, hold on to my tail and whatever you do, don't let go and don't look down."

The long climb began slowly, but Kiwi soon gathered momentum and the strange journey sped up. In the dark, the kittens could feel a draught of cold air coming down from the top of the chute. It made their fur stick up in crazy directions. Nearer and nearer they moved towards the top, higher and higher, squinting in the dark.

James thought the chute resembled a curly straw, travelling up the middle of the narrow, stone shaft. Clinging to the walls were hundreds of cobwebs, upon which tiny black spiders scurried back and forth, busily spinning their little homes.

Up and up the three friends went. Amy and James clung on with all their might, and were careful not to look down. Higher and higher, and then Kiwi stopped. To the right was a ledge that appeared to lead off to a doorway in the wall. "Take a look at that," she said, puffing a little.

"Eh?" muttered Amy and James, who looked down simultaneously and then seriously regretted it. "Ahhhhhh!" they gasped.

Suspended in the air by only a furry tail.

"Ahhhhhh!"

"No, not down there," said Kiwi. "Look over here, at the door!" Clenching her teeth, she increased her grip on the chute. The kittens were wriggling far too much and she hoped she didn't slide down.

Amy slowly opened her eyes and peeked at the ledge. Great, she thought, when she spied solid ground, but there was a gap between them and it, and a long, long way down. "W-we're not, are w-we?" she stammered.

"Where's your sense of adventure?" asked Kiwi.

Amy looked at James, who looked at Amy, who looked at James. They sighed. When you're suspended halfway up a stone shaft across a slippery chute, hanging on to someone else's tail for your life, you're not in a good position to argue.

"Let's find out where that meow came from last night," said Kiwi. "All you have to do is concentrate and remember you are not human in this world. You're cats, and cats are the best jumpers. Well, except for kangaroos, who I think are the best. I met one once and he… Well, I'm wandering off the point. To cut a long story short, I'm going to shimmy up this shaft until I'm level with that ledge and then we are going to jump on…"

"Bu-bu-but," stammered the kittens.

"BOOOOO!"

Amy and James jumped out of their skins – "Ahhh" – but, whooosh, they flew through the air, glided and made a smooth landing on the ledge. "Wow, we did it," they cheered and did a little cat dance, followed by some purrs.

Kiwi landed beside them. "There's no time to lose. Quit with the boogie. Let's go!"

The three of them crept along the stone ledge, which was the exact width of their bodies – cat size. It eeled its way along the wall and stopped at a doorway.

"A doorway," remarked James.

"Ten out of ten for observation," said Kiwi, who ran straight in.

"Nerves of steel," mumbled Amy.

"You don't think she's just a bit mad?" asked James.

"I heard that!" called Kiwi. "Hurry up!"

I think I preferred it when she couldn't talk, thought James.

The two kittens bounced through the doorway and found themselves in a long corridor, lit by a single, yellow bulb.

"That's very odd," said Kiwi.

Amy looked around, but couldn't see anything unusual. "What is?"

"That's not a cat bulb," said Kiwi, pointing upwards with her tail.

"So?"

"We only have cat bulbs in Cat City," she explained. "Blue is the best light for our eyes. Cats see better in it. Other colours can give us a headache. This one gives off a yellow light and it isn't shaped like a cat's eye. That means it wasn't made in Cat City. I've never seen one like that before."

Giving a quizzical look, Kiwi carried on walking. The corridor turned and turned again, like a maze, lit by yellow lights. Suddenly, it came to an abrupt end and a yellow door. "Shall we open it?" she asked.

The kittens nodded and jumped behind the black cat as she pushed the door. It creaked open with an eerie sigh, squeaking on its hinges as if it had not been touched for a while. A metallic, spiral staircase stood before them. Amy and James looked at one another with a mixture of raw fear and wild excitement.

"Here we go," said Kiwi, scampering up.

"Here we go again," said Amy, following.

James was last, doing his big bunny hops up the stairs. Five minutes later, all three stood panting, feeling out of breath and a little dizzy in a room without any windows. Ahead was a solitary cat flap. Kiwi pushed it open and peered inside. There was a sheer drop – a long way down below was a massive room. Stretching across from the cat flap was a metal walkway, about the width of a cat and no more, and it led all the way across to a metal ladder, which led down to the ground. Beams stuck out along the ceiling.

"What can you see?" Amy asked Kiwi from behind her black, bushy tail.

"Looks like a warehouse, but we're too high up for me to see properly."

Kiwi slid forwards until her whole body disappeared through the cat flap. It closed behind her. Amy and James nodded to one another and poked their heads out of the flap, not wanting to miss anything exciting. They spotted Kiwi straight away, slinking quietly across the metal walkway. Then they glanced down, but it was a very long way to the bottom where numerous cats were loading boxes into crates, which were being moved around. Lines upon lines of cats worked in silence while the machinery hummed loudly. The kittens backed up, pulling their heads through the cat flap, and sat down in the corridor.

"What do you think is going on in there?" asked Amy.

James shrugged. "They're just packing biscuits."

"With all that machinery? And everyone is quiet and not talking – that's unlike the catizens here."

"I have a weird feeling," said James.

Just then Kiwi poked her nose through the cat flap. "What are you two up to?"

"Nothing," said James.

"Waiting for you," Amy added.

"Well," whispered Kiwi, "it would be kitty nice if you'd come along this walkway with me. There's another cat flap at the end, which we could explore. There's a ladder going down, too, but I think that would be a bad idea."

"Mmm, it's good you realise that would be bad," said Amy.

"Don't you think it might be dangerous to go across?" asked James.

Kiwi thought for a moment. "Maybe, maybe not. At the first sign of trouble, I promise I'll be zapping Furrball on my catpad."

The kittens were quiet.

"Of course, you can wait here if you want," Kiwi suggested. Although the kittens seemed scared, she knew no harm would come to them while crossing the beam. Cats had supreme balance after all, and the catizens working below would not be able to hear them. She thought it might boost her friends' confidence, and perhaps help James to defeat his vertigo once and for all.

Kiwi lifted the cat flap with her head and the two kittens stepped through. The long, metal beam stretched ahead of them and, sure enough, at the far end was a small cat flap. It looked very far away. James moved his head to peer downwards, but Kiwi nudged him with the tip of her nose. Perhaps it was best not to look, he thought.

Keeping his eyes focused on the cat flap in the distance, James put one paw in front of the other, held his breath and stepped on to the beam with his funny cat body. Then he put the other paw down, followed by the next, and so it went. James felt weirdly, but completely balanced, and he could feel his tail rising in the air behind him. It was perfect and he no longer felt scared. "Wow!" he whispered to himself. There was no way he could have ever done this as a human! Now it was dead easy. He stuck his pink nose in the air and strutted along with confidence.

Amy stared wide-eyed in shock. "He makes it look so simple."

"That's because it is," said Kiwi. "I keep reminding you that you're a cat now. Think like one. This kind of thing is second nature."

James heard the soft pad of Amy's paws on the beam behind him and he guessed that Kiwi was not far away either. Without turning to look, he kept on walking slowly and surely with a calm focus. From below, the whirr and hum of machinery crept up into the air. But it seemed to be coming from a long way away; a land far distant from the metal beam up in the rafters. The tiny cat flap at the opposite end of the warehouse grew bigger and bigger until it touched James' whiskers. Still careful not to look behind him, he pushed open the flap and crept into the space beyond.

Soon, three pairs of whiskers had emerged through the flap and were walking along another long passageway, lit by a yellow light, which split in two directions.

"Left or right?" Kiwi asked.

"Left," said James.

"Right," said Amy.

"Okay, I'll follow my nose," said Kiwi, striding off to the right. Amy grinned and pounced after her. The passageway carried on around a corner and ended at a concrete slope. It led down and down, around and around, like the spiral staircase. There were neither windows nor lights, only gloom, and the kittens were relieved to be able to see in the dark.

"This is kind of creepy," said Amy.

James grinned. "But exciting."

"Weirdo!"

James giggled, knowing she was joking.

Kiwi stopped. "Shush, we don't want anyone to hear us. I've no idea where we're going or what we'll find when we get there. If someone sees us, they might not be too happy about us wandering around without a permit."

"No permit?" asked James.

"Nope," said Kiwi. "I hate paperwork."

"Now she tells us," sighed Amy.

They carried on walking down the concrete

slope, which came to an abrupt end in front of a blue, wooden cat flap. Kiwi nudged it open and shot inside. Amy and James followed. They found themselves in a large cellar with stone walls. All around were bottles and crates piled high. At one side was a lift and at the other was yet another passageway.

"I think the lift might take us back up to that warehouse we walked across," said Kiwi.

James pointed to the crates. "They've got stickers on, saying Catskins Biscuits, but that one has some small holes in the side."

Kiwi bounded over and curled a claw under the lid. The kittens did the same and together they flicked off the lid. Empty.

"That's odd," Kiwi remarked.

Amy scratched her head. "What?"

Kiwi leapt into the crate.

Maybe there were biscuit crumbs inside, thought James. Yummy, unless they were made of mice, and then super yuck.

Kiwi started sniffing and clawing. Splinters of wood flew out of the box. "Aha, just as I thought – look!"

The kittens stood up on their hind legs and peered into the crate. Kiwi blinked and shook the dust off her face. She had made a hole in the bottom of the crate, but it wasn't the real bottom at all. Inside the hole was a space large enough to hide something, but what?

"Who knows what they're putting in there," said Kiwi, jumping out. "Let's hide this box and tidy up."

They pushed the lid back in place and nudged the

crate into a corner, behind some others, so no-one would find it for a while. Hopefully, a long while, thought Kiwi.

"Should we tell Inspector Furrball?" asked Amy.

"I don't know," said Kiwi. "I'm not sure what's going on here. There's something fishy about this place. It's like a maze. First we have to find out who receives these deliveries and what goes in them."

Just then there was a rumble from the lift shaft.

"Quick, run! Someone's coming!" hissed Kiwi, racing across the cellar floor towards the passageway. They all ran as fast as they could, skidding around the corner, and on and on in the almost darkness. Amy and James huffed and puffed on their short legs to keep up with Kiwi, who sped along smoothly. At the end of the corridor was a small door. Kiwi charged into it and it sprung open. Chilly air hit their faces. They were outside the building. The cold made the kittens sneeze, but they were safe. They sat down with relief and puffed.

"That was close," Amy muttered.

"You can say that again," said James and he started purring, almost naturally.

Chapter 12: Special delivery

"We need to check out the delivery destinations for all of the companies in Cat City," said Kiwi.

Siam stopped tapping his keyboard and nodded. "Sure. I can get you a list in a few minutes."

"We'll be over there," she added, getting a bowl of milk from the vending machine.

It was quite a long list as there were about a hundred companies in Cat City, all run by catizens employing cat workers and making different things. The city was pretty self-sufficient and everyone had a job. One of the biggest companies was Catskins.

"Here we go," said Kiwi. "Wow, they deliver to a lot of catizens. Nearly everyone seems to buy their biscuits."

"Even Cat Crime has them!" Amy purred, pointing to the milk machine. Alongside all of the bowls were mini bags of biscuits.

"Right, so I guess we should check out all of these companies," Kiwi continued.

Amy looked puzzled. "Why not check out the deliveries here, seeing as we are sitting right inside one of their customers?"

"Yeah," said James, looking up from his bowl of milk with liquid dripping off his whiskers. He moved his head suddenly and cold milk flicked across the faces of Amy and Kiwi. "Oops," he mumbled, looking sheepish.

Amy simply blinked at him.

"Siam, where do Cat Crime's deliveries come in?" asked Kiwi, licking James' present off her face.

"At the delivery depot on the ground floor, at the back of the building, of course," the Siamese answered. "There's a new catizen down there now. Kip used to deal with the deliveries until... well... until he disappeared. You'll need a pass, so take mine. Just remember to bring it back!"

"Okay," said Kiwi, taking the red and gold ticket. "I guess you two better wait here. I'll be back as soon as I can."

"I'll keep them amused," said Siam. "I'll show them the latest version of Cat-tris."

"See you soon," called out Kiwi, trotting off to the delivery depot. So, Kip had been checking in the deliveries before he vanished? She wondered if there was a connection – maybe he came across something he shouldn't have. She swiped her pass through the security lock and breezed into the depot.

"Name and business?" asked the skinny, brown-and-white striped catizen in a red cap and waistcoat. His name badge said Stripey.

"Detective Kiwi."

"Do you have a pass?" asked the unimpressed cat with a piercing stare.

"Yes, here it is. Inspector Furrball asked me to investigate down here, so you can check with him."

"I will," replied Stripey sharply. He turned and spoke into his catpad in a shifty manner, but soon turned back with a satisfied smile. "You can go through. Do you have any questions?"

"Where are the deliveries from Catskins?"

Stripey laughed. "Ah, very special business that. You just want to sneak some extra goodies. Well, Detective, we had a delivery yesterday – you'll find them right over there! The crates are in alphabetical order."

"Thanks," smiled Kiwi, hiding her irritation. She trotted off with her tail in the air before she said something she might regret. Bouncing across the depot, she checked the crates stacked under 'C', and soon found three from Catskins. Someone had a sweet tooth and she imagined it was Furrball!

Kiwi glanced back at the brown-and-white cat. He was reading a magazine – she recognised the cover of *Fishing Monthly* – with his paws propped up on his desk. She flicked out a sharp claw and lifted the lid off one of the crates. Inside were neat piles of colourfully wrapped biscuits. The fishy aroma wafted up. Kiwi took them all out of the crate carefully and laid them on the floor. Behind her, Stripey was still engrossed in his magazine, his face hidden by his cap.

Kiwi leapt into the crate and scratched away at the wood. Just as she suspected – it had a false bottom! As quietly as possible, she scratched and scraped until she made a hole. Then she froze. She hadn't expected to find *that*. Who would deliver such a thing here? She buzzed a number on her catpad and whispered, "Furrball, I think you should come and take a look at this."

Kiwi sat down and waited.

When the inspector arrived, he rubbed his furry chin and frowned. "This is most extraordinary," he said. "We should keep this a secret. No-one needs to know about it. Help me to carry this crate up to my office and I'll lock it away in a cupboard. Perhaps I should cancel all of Catskins' deliveries?"

"That would arouse suspicion," said Kiwi.

"That's true. I will ask for all of the Catskins crates to be delivered to my office. They will think I have a biscuit addiction, which won't arouse any suspicion," said Furrball, laughing. "Although some catizens will probably start advising me to go to the cat gym!"

"I was wondering what their plan was," said Kiwi in a serious tone. "The missing catizens case is more important, but I want to find out what's going on at the Catskins factory. Perhaps I should arrange an interview with the owner."

"I think that's a kitty good idea," said Furrball, rubbing his eyes. "But be careful and take Paws with you."

"Do I have to?"

Furrball nodded. "It's the only way he's going to learn. We all had to start somewhere and he is my nephew. I have a responsibility to his late mother. I'll make a detective out of him yet!"

"Okay," sighed Kiwi, her tail drooping. She failed to see any family resemblance at all.

Chapter 13: The interview

Mr J Catskins hobbled into his office, gripping a rickety walking stick. He was a very old, grey catizen with fading eyes, in front of which perched a wobbly pair of metal spectacles. Most of his whiskers were missing and his green waistcoat had seen better days. "Good morning and please sit down. I will ask for some fresh milk to be sent up. Cookies anyone?" he asked, welcoming Kiwi, Amy and James.

He shuffled around the room, making sure his guests were comfortably seated on the plush cushions arranged on the floor around a circular table. A variety of cat toys sat in a bowl on top of it. Eventually, once he was sure everyone else was fine, he took a seat behind his desk. "So, how can I help you?" he asked.

Kiwi glanced over at the rather large, ginger 'bouncer' catizen standing by the door. His big, muscular front legs were folded across his chest and he stood up on his hind legs, his tail flicking with annoyance. One of the tomcat's ears was missing and one of his eyes was half shut. He wasn't pretty.

Kiwi looked quickly back at Mr J Catskins. "We're doing door-to-door interviews regarding the recent catnappings," she said, placing a small recording device on the table. It was blue, shaped like a cat's eye and blinked.

"Oh yes," replied the old cat, wiping his whiskers. "I've read about that in the *Morning Meow* – five isn't it?"

"Six now."

"That's a lot," said Mr J Catskins. "Do you have any idea where they are?"

"That's what we're trying to find out. I was wondering if you recognised any of the missing catizens." Kiwi pushed a sheet of paper, bearing a list of names and six little cat faces, across the table.

"I don't recognise any of them."

"Take your time – there's no rush."

"No, I'm certain I've never seen any of them before," said the old cat, "although my memory isn't what it once was."

"Okay," said Kiwi. "Have you noticed anything out of the ordinary in the past month? Seen anything strange?"

"No."

"Have any of your workers disappeared?"

"No."

"Have any customers suddenly cancelled orders?"

"No."

"Have any of your workers been acting strangely?" Kiwi tried not to glance at the angry looking bouncer.

"No."

"Has anyone new started working here?"

"No."

"Have you made any unusual deliveries outside Cat City?"

Mr J Catskins raised an eyebrow. "No."

"Have any unusual deliveries come here from outside Cat City?"

"Of course not," snapped the old, grey cat. "We run a respectable business."

Kiwi noticed the big, ginger tom shuffling impatiently. He was staring straight at her. She gulped. He had rather large muscles. "I mean, have you received any strange deliveries from anywhere outside the city? We cannot rule out the possibility that the missing catizens are no longer here in Cat City. Maybe someone from outside…"

"I don't think I can help you," said Mr J Catskins, rising to his paws. "There has not been anything unusual at all."

The room fell silent. You could have cut the atmosphere with a rather sharp claw.

"Do you know your company is the richest in the city?" Kiwi asked.

"No, I didn't, but it is gratifying to know. We work very hard," said the old cat. "You must excuse me as it's time for my nap. I'm not a kitten any more, you know."

Kiwi stood, deciding to change tactics. "I

understand you bought the company a year ago?"

"Yes."

"From…"

"Madame Purrfect."

"Her family ran the company for a very long time, didn't they?" asked Kiwi. "Why did she sell?"

Mr J Catskins paused. "Yes, that is true, but I think she was tired of it. She wanted a change. She said she was going to visit relatives who lived by the sea. I can't remember where. She was thinking of retiring and wanted to do some things first – visit new places… She had no-one to pass the business on to – no family, you see, so she decided to sell. For quite a lot of money I might add."

"Do you know where Madame Purrfect is now?" asked Kiwi.

"You're the detective! I fail to see what this has to do with the missing catizens."

"I'm just pursuing all of my lines of enquiry," said Kiwi calmly. "You understand…"

"Yes, yes, but I'm a very busy man, Miss."

"Detective Kiwi."

"Yes, *Detective* Kiwi, and now Ginger will see you out."

The big, ginger tomcat crunched his paws together and flexed his muscles. "This way," he grunted. He liked showing catizens out.

Chapter 14: Paint it red

"Excuse the mess, but we've got the decorators in. They're doing the whole building, floor by floor," said Inspector Furrball, showing Kiwi and her two little friends into his office.

"Oh," said James, "does that mean they're going to paint this ugly building a nicer colour?"

Furrball laughed. "No, it will always be grey... and maybe one day I'll tell you why."

James frowned, sure there could not possibly be a good reason.

"Anyway, inside it's all going to be red," said the inspector, his eyes lighting up. "A brighter red... well, redder."

"I like red," said Amy. "It's a happy colour."

"Indeed. Any luck with the investigation?"

Amy blushed, feeling very important to have been asked. "We met this really scary bouncer called Ginger, with a lot of muscles and a torn ear. He looked like he had been in a lot of fights – and won them!"

"Even Kiwi was scared of him," James chipped in.

Kiwi's ears went back. "Was not..."

"Was too..."

"Anyway, we didn't learn much," said Kiwi, sitting down and curling her tail around her. "Mr J Catskins was rather uncooperative."

Furrball looked surprised.

"He didn't like answering questions," said Amy, batting a jingling ball across the floor. She stopped, filled with embarrassment when she realised what she was doing and pretended to scratch.

"That's interesting. Any leads?"

"Well… no. None. Zero to be exact," said Kiwi. "Mr J Catskins did say Madame Purrfect left Cat City to stay with relatives by the sea. Could you check that?"

"How odd. I heard that she went on a cruise. I'll get Siam on to it straight away. I always did like Madame Purrfect. Such a nice ladycat," Furrball sighed, gazing off into the distance.

James tutted and Amy raised her eyes to the ceiling. Kiwi coughed.

Furrball dropped his pen. "Ah, anyway," he said, "maybe you should search the Catskins building and investigate further there. I can get you an entry permit."

"Okay," replied Kiwi, shushing the kittens before they could say they had already entered the building without a permit! "That sounds like a kitty good idea. Can you find out if Mr J Catskins kept the same workers when he bought the factory? We need as much information on him as possible."

"And Ginger," piped up Amy.

"Yes, why not him too?" Kiwi agreed. "There's definitely something fishy going on in that building and it's not just the smell of the biscuits. We'll be off now."

"Right, be careful," said Furrball, showing them to the door.

"Ooooops… noooooo," hissed James, tripping over a bucket of paint.

The inspector guffawed loudly. "A red paw

looks very fetching! But, I hope they'll have finished painting by the end of the week, so I can have my old office back. Otherwise the whole of you will be red!"

"And we'll be calling you Ginger, Jimster," giggled Amy in a catty splutter.

"Oh, Furrball, by the way, did you tell anyone about the crate I found here?" asked Kiwi when the kittens scampered away towards the lift.

"No, and it is locked away," he whispered. "Don't worry."

The kittens' ears perked up as their hearing had improved a lot. They turned around. "What crate?" Amy asked.

"Nothing," purred Kiwi, winking at the inspector. "We were talking about fish-eye stuffed dates."

"Yuck!"

Chapter 15: The factory tour

"Come on, Paws!" Kiwi meowed. "It's not much further. We should hurry before the sun goes down and curfew starts."

"Okay, okay," he replied, unwrapping yet another sandwich. "I'm just hungry. I forgot to have my breakfast!"

"But it's the afternoon," James whispered to Amy.

"Did you remember to bring the permit?" asked Kiwi.

"P-permit?" stammered Paws.

"Yes, to enter the building."

"Oh, that permit…"

Kiwi put her paws on her head. "You've forgotten it, haven't you?" she growled, turning to confront Paws.

"W-well, no, I didn't f-forget it."

"So, you've got it?" asked Kiwi, relieved.

"No… I just failed to remember it, that's all," said the clumsy Paws, ducking Kiwi's paw swipe.

"So where is it?" she hissed.

"Back with Uncle Furrball!"

"Geeeeez!" exclaimed Kiwi, knocking Paws' sandwich into the dirt. He pouted and scrambled to retrieve the best bits.

An hour later, on their second attempt that afternoon, the two cats and two kittens returned to the building. Kiwi made sure she was carrying the permit and that Paws didn't have any sandwiches to distract him. The factory had a long, cobbled drive, which swept upwards from the iron railings

77

to a big entrance. It looked quite grand for a factory.

"This is a much posher entrance than the alley," said Amy with wide eyes.

The old, stone building had three floors. Gargoyles in the shape of fish heads with bulging eyeballs gazed down from above the windows. Kiwi rang the bell, which hung on a very long chain, and waited. The heavy, wooden door was opened by a friendly looking cat, and not Ginger, whom everyone had half-expected to see come roaring down the driveway.

"Hello there, I'm Mr Dogg," announced the skinny, brown cat, who was wearing little black boots and a black cap. Amy and James stared in astonishment.

"Hello," said Kiwi politely. "I have a permit from Mayor Tom to view this factory. I came to interview Mr J Catskins the other day."

"Let me see," said Mr Dogg, studying the permit. "Oh, that looks fine. I can show you around. I just need to tell Mr J Catskins first."

The door slammed with a clang and the cats found themselves in a brightly coloured hallway with an emerald green carpet. There were two doors, one to the right and one to the left, and straight ahead a huge, wooden staircase stretched upwards. Kiwi noticed with a smile that the light bulbs were regulation blue.

"This is a cool place," said James, nudging Amy.

"Very different from the parts we explored," she whispered.

"What a massive staircase," said James loudly. "And look at all these pictures of catizens with moustaches and old hats with feathers and stuff – they must be very old. They look like they've stepped out of a history book."

"They are all the past owners of the factory, in order," announced Mr Dogg, appearing suddenly. The others jumped and turned around. "I've checked with Mr J Catskins and he has agreed that I can show you around. He is too busy to do it himself. I'm sure you won't mind, no?"

"That's fine," purred Kiwi, flashing her eyes.

Mr Dogg went bright red and adjusted his cap.

James stopped in front of the last in the line of pictures. "This must be Madame Purrfect," he said, pointing to a picture of a sleek, rather attractive, blue Burmese catizen with soft, grey eyes and a white feather boa. A necklace with a fish-shaped, red stone glittered around her neck. "No wonder old Furrball keeps gawping out of windows whenever her name is said," he whispered to his sister.

"Wow," muttered Amy.

"Yes," said Mr Dogg sternly. "That is the previous owner of the factory. She retired a year ago."

"Did you know her?" asked Kiwi.

"No," he replied, "but I heard she was a real beauty. I started working here after Mr J Catskins took over. Oh excuse me," he sighed as the phone on the wall began to meow.

Amy and James stared. It was meowing?!

So, Mr Catskins was wrong – not all of his employees have worked here for years, thought Kiwi.

"Hello?" said Mr Dogg. "Yes, I see. No problem."

Replacing the handset, he instructed the waiting cats to "follow me". They walked up the staircase with its green-painted floorboards to a wide landing, which was really a gigantic room swathed in an emerald green carpet. In the corner stood a mini catbar and numerous squishy, green cushions were scattered around the floor. Amy noticed a few cat toys dotted about and a scratching post, which she had a sudden urge to use. It was funny how such things were beginning to seem normal.

"This is where we entertain guests and company visitors," explained Mr Dogg. Kiwi noted the blue lights. Nothing unusual here.

There were three doors at the end of the landing: one white, one yellow and one green, all with gold-coloured handles. Mr Dogg opened the yellow one first, which led into a room full of yellow cat litter trays, along with cat-size sinks and dryers. The room smelt of fish. "We like to keep it smelling sweet in here," he explained.

At the far end was a row of cubicles. A ladycat sat in the middle of the room, offering a range of perfumes, snacks and ribbons.

"This is the bathroom with all new facilities – unisex, you know. It's the latest thing and no-one has complained yet," said Mr Dogg. "We have shower cubicles, but we find most catizens prefer the self-wash. I guess old habits die hard!"

Amy and James stared in disbelief – no-one was ever going to believe this! Paws trundled along behind, munching on a snack he got in the bathroom. When he dropped the wrapper on the floor, James scooped it up and put it in a bin.

"Okay, moving on – through the green door, I can show you where our famous cat biscuits are made and packed for sale," said Mr Dogg, smiling proudly.

"What about the white door?" James whispered to his sister.

"Shush," she hissed, pushing him forwards. "We'll probably see it later."

The group followed a green line painted along the wooden floor, which cut straight across a massive, high-walled room. All around, machines buzzed and hummed, and rattled and whirred. Cats dressed in little white hats, aprons, gloves and socks rushed around busily. No-one chatted – there was too much to do.

A cat-radio sang out from somewhere. Amy realised she could make out lots of faint mewing and the odd purr, strangely in tune. She blinked in astonishment. "Look!" she said to James, pointing at the workers. "They're all wearing cute little white socks!"

James nodded, suddenly missing his own socks, especially the cartoon ones.

Mr Dogg overheard. "They are worn for hygiene. We don't want any extra ingredients in our goodies!"

In one corner of the room was a big mixer, into which some cats were pouring various unknown ingredients. The giant machine whirred and whirred, and a tube emerged from the side, which passed along into another mixer, into which other cats were adding more ingredients. The mixer whizzed and spun very fast. James felt dizzy watching it and nearly fell over his tail. Splodges of mixture plopped out of the end of a pipe on to a wide conveyor belt, which whizzed along into an oven, and then whizzed out again and under a presser to be cut into shapes.

"Wow," said James, rushing over to look at the end result – the familiar looking, fish-shaped Catskins Biscuits, still warm. Their scrumptious aroma wafted up his nostrils.

"What's in them?" asked Amy as they sped past her eyes.

Mr Dogg laughed. "That's a very old – and very secret – recipe. It's even a mystery to us workers."

A hush fell over the kittens. Top secret? Wow!

"No! Please don't touch!" meowed Mr Dogg, bouncing on his little black booties towards Paws, who was standing dangerously close to the conveyor belt of perfectly warm goodies. "You can have some when we get to the packing section. And please try not to dribble!"

"Yum, free food," said James happily, as Paws strode off grumbling to himself.

The group followed the green-painted line onwards as the conveyor belt whizzed past into the next room where the biscuits cooled in neat lines. Cats swiftly wrapped them, while others placed the final product on yet another conveyor belt that sped onwards. Mr Dogg stopped and inspected the process, and then picked up four packets of freshly wrapped biscuits. He handed one to each of his visitors, saying, "Now, don't eat them all at once," before leading the way towards the next room.

Dawdling behind the others, the loud crunching of Paws' never-tiring jaws could be heard above the whizzing and whirring of the machines!

"Right, this is the packing room," announced

Mr Dogg. All around, cats dressed in white gloves and boots packed biscuits into crates and dragged them in wheelbarrows to a lift at the far side of the room. Amy looked up and nudged James. Up above they could see the metal beam they had crossed previously after overcoming their fear. Now it looked easy to both of them.

"Where does the lift go?" asked Kiwi.

"To the cellar and the two upper floors," said Mr Dogg. "We'll go to the cellar next. The upstairs floors are the owner's private residence."

Amy glanced around the packing room, but there were no other doors. They all crept into the lift, which rushed down with a whoosh, shuddered, shook and stopped with a mighty bump. Ouch! They all stumbled to their four paws and wobbled out. Kiwi sighed – Cat City lifts were just so embarrassing.

"This is the cellar," Mr Dogg announced. "Here we store all of our crates for delivery, and over here is the delivery hatch."

He approached what resembled a giant cat flap and pressed a green button on the wall. The hatch opened with a loud, whirring noise to reveal a small car park outside, where three green vans were parked. Their sides were emblazoned with the words 'Catskins Biscuits, Cat City's Oldest and Best' in big, gold lettering. A driver sat in one of the vans, dressed in a bright green uniform, reading the *Morning Meow*.

"Right, catizens, that was the grand tour," said Mr Dogg, rubbing his paws together. "Shall I take you back to the entrance?"

Kiwi hesitated. "What is in those crates?"

"Biscuits, of course," said Mr Dogg. "What else?"

Kiwi paused. "Can I open one?"

Mr Dogg looked amazed. "Of course," he said, opening one with his claw. "If you could help me with the lid... thank you. Take a look inside, if you like."

"What are you looking for?" asked Paws, who kept burping loudly from eating far too many fishy cookies.

James turned his nose away.

"Just checking," said Kiwi. "I'm sure everything is fine, but I have to check these things."

She then unpacked the entire case, to the astonishment of Mr Dogg, and peered inside. How odd, she thought – everything looked normal and the crate did not have a false bottom. Pretending she was not surprised, she carefully replaced the biscuits one by one.

"Well," Kiwi said, cheerfully, "everything seems to be in order. Thank you for showing us around, Mr Dogg. We have many other companies to check, so we should be on our way. I hope you understand that we have to search the entire city for the missing catizens. I guess you've read the *Morning Meow* and know all about it. Please tell Mr J Catskins this. At Cat Crime, we like to keep good relations with all catizens."

"I will," said Mr Dogg, smiling back. "I hope you've had a most enjoyable visit. It was my pleasure to show you around. Any questions before you go?"

"Erm, do you have any more free samples?"

asked Paws, wiping some crumbs off his nose. "You know, for police purposes, of course!"

The kittens sighed.

Chapter 16: Back at Cat Crime

"Where's Paws?" asked Inspector Furrball when the intrepid trio returned to Cat Crime. They were sitting in one of the spare offices while the decorators finished painting the inspector's room, and the seating was nowhere near as comfortable.

"He had to go home because he had a stomach ache," said Amy, wriggling on her cushion in a bid to get comfy.

"He ate too much," explained James, sliding on to the floor by accident. "He kept stuffing his face with cookies."

"Oh dear, I'm afraid he has a very big appetite," said the inspector with a sigh. "I keep trying to get him to eat less and get fit, go to the cat-gym or at least go to the races to chase a few mice..."

Amy and James screwed up their noses.

"... but it's no use. I can't force him. He's going to be quite unfit when it comes to chasing bad catizens when he's out on cat patrol," Furrball sighed.

Kiwi handed the inspector a free sample of Catskins Biscuits and a leaflet showing pictures of the inside of the factory. "We visited the building. That's the promotional brochure. We were shown the rooms that visitors see. Strangely, I checked a crate in the cellar that was to be delivered and it didn't have a false bottom."

"So, either they had hidden away the false-bottomed ones or most of the crates are alright. Maybe most of the deliveries are okay and only a few are dodgy," said Furrball, stroking his whiskers.

"Which arouses more suspicion as to why the crates delivered here were…"

"Yes," agreed Furrball. "Perhaps we should check out the other places that order Catskins Biscuits and see if their crates have been tampered with. Even the mayor gets them!"

The kittens looked at each other. What on earth was in that crate? They were so curious to know.

"In the factory there was a room with a white door that Mr Dogg didn't show us into," said Amy, jumping up, her tail whipping across her brother's face.

James wrinkled up his nose and sneezed. "And the light bulbs were regulation cat bulbs," he added, sneezing again.

"The relevance being?" asked Furrball, confused.

Amy explained: "When we visited the building the first time…"

"The first time?" The inspector stared straight at Kiwi.

"Eh, yes," the black cat mumbled. "I was going to mention that…"

Furrball frowned.

Amy continued, "When we visited the first time, we explored some old rooms and corridors that were lit by non-cat bulbs, giving off a yellow light."

"There were many cat flaps, too," added Kiwi.

Inspector Furrball was surprised. "That's strange. We don't use cat flaps any more. They are very un-PC. And those old-style bulbs are banned. Catizens cannot see as well in yellow light. Blue is best. All blue bulbs are made by one company, kittens, and we don't import them. However, the factory is probably the oldest in Cat City, which would explain the cat flaps, but the bulbs are another matter. Why haven't they changed them?" Furrball scratched his nose.

There was silence while everyone thought about it.

"What should we do?" James asked after a few minutes.

"I think you should press on with investigating the deliveries of Catskins Biscuits. This is a difficult situation though – we don't want to arouse Mr J Catskins' suspicions," added Furrball.

"We'll say we are investigating the disappearances," said Kiwi. "Talking of which, how is the case going?"

The inspector shook his head. "Not very well."

"I haven't seen anything in the *Morning Meow*," said Kiwi. "That's good news."

"Yes, it's true that there haven't been any more disappearances," said Furrball, "but we received a ransom note."

"Really? This is the first I've heard."

"I didn't want to concern you – we only got it yesterday," said Furrball. "I didn't want to divert you from the Catskins case. But the ransom note moves the catnapping case forward – now we have something to go on."

Kiwi was curious. Why had the note arrived so late, after so many catizens had gone missing? "What did it say?"

"They want a million Cat Bills in unmarked notes within two weeks. We have a paw-writing specialist on the case and we're checking some new lines of enquiry that Siam's computer checks brought up. But

I want you to concentrate on Catskins and find out what is going on there," Furrball insisted.

"Okay," said Kiwi. "I'll ask Siam to check the computer for Catskins' orders for this week. We'll get on to it straight away."

"Report back here tomorrow. And good luck."

Chapter 17: Undercover

The following afternoon, Inspector Furrball showed Kiwi and the kittens into his office before buzzing Miss Kitty to bring some refreshments. "You'll be glad to know the painting is finished," he said. "Well, on this floor anyway. It smells of paint, but it's all done. It's great to be back in my office."

The kittens pounced on the big, comfy, red cushions and rolled around until Miss Kitty brought in some saucers of fresh milk. Their ears perked up and their noses twitched, and they lapped it all up, managing to keep the liquid in their bowls this time. As it was such a hot day, Miss Kitty handed out seconds.

"We investigated eight companies off a delivery list of 20. We found no dubious crates," said Kiwi. "As far as I can tell, the only dodgy one wound up here at Cat Crime. We'll check the other companies over the next few days."

Amy sat up straight all of a sudden, feeling the fur on her back stand on end. "What's that scratching noise?"

"Oh no, not again!" whined Furrball. "It must be mice. We have to lay some more traps."

"Bu-but," stammered James. "I like mice, you can't trap them. I have a hamster at home... his name is Hammy."

Kiwi's eyes nearly popped out. "Erm, Jimster means he likes mice, Furrball. He gets his words confused sometimes, being a very young kitten."

James covered his mouth with his paw.

Furrball smiled, having no idea what a hamster was. "We're not going to kill them. I promise we'll catch the mice and nothing bad will happen to them. They do taste scrumptious in a pie though."

James' mouth dropped open and Amy suddenly went off her milk. Poor little mice!

***

After investigating some other companies that ordered Catskins Biscuits and finding nothing, the three adventurers wandered the streets of Cat City. It really was the hottest day they had ever experienced. "Let's get some sweets or ice cream," suggested Amy.

"As long as it isn't from Mrs Ebenry!" said James pouting.

"Or we could go to the Catema," said Kiwi. "It's showing *Cats and Dogs, Artificial Catelligence* and *For a Few Kitties More*."

The kittens giggled.

"Hey, look! There's Paws over there," said Amy.

"Where?"

"Over there!"

"What's he doing? Stuffing his face again?" James laughed.

"I don't think so," said Kiwi. "He's in between those trees over there, talking to a skinny, black cat with a missing ear and wearing a black waistcoat."

"I see him," Amy answered.

Kiwi watched the black cat give Paws a box and wander away.

"That's odd," James remarked.

"Perhaps it's a present – or food," Amy said, giggling.

Kiwi carried on watching as Paws walked off down the hill. "Perhaps he has a lead in the catnapping case."

"I guess we're not going to the Catema then?" James sighed, having thought it would be fun to go to a cat cinema. Did the movies star cats? Imagine!

"Are we going to follow him?" asked Amy.

Kiwi nodded. "I think we are, but let's do it secretly. I don't want Paws to get nervous if he is on to something. He might need backup – so we're it! Let's walk on opposite sides of the road. You two cross over and walk ten paces behind me at a distance. Keep to the shadows, but keep me in sight. Meow if you're in trouble!"

"Wow, surveillance," said James. "Very James Bond. Come on, Miss Moneypenny!"

"I'm not Moneypenny," argued Amy, following her brother across the road. "You're Doctor Evil!"

"Who?" Kiwi shrugged and started walking. She could just make out Furrball's nephew wandering ahead, carrying the small box. Kiwi kept a close eye on Paws as she followed him down the hill and across Cat City. Behind her, on the opposite side of the road, the two kittens crept along secretly and silently. The four figures strode down streets and alleys, across roads and between buildings as the orange sun sank lower in the sky.

Over an hour later, with the kittens' paws aching, the three investigators stopped and hid behind a wall as Paws, quite a distance ahead of them, strode up to the Catskins building. He didn't knock at the front door though – he went around to the secluded back entrance.

"What's he up to?" whispered James.

"I don't know," Kiwi whispered back. "He's undercover, so maybe Furrball has given him a secret mission."

"Or maybe he's sneaking in for some more free samples," said Amy.

"We could follow him and ask what he's up to," James suggested.

"That's a plan and a half," said Kiwi, "but a tricky one. I'll buzz Furrball on my catpad and tell him we're going into the building, just in case we need backup. It will give him time to arrange another permit. Are you two up to this? It's been a long day."

"Yes," they replied, excited. Their tails swished and their whiskers perked up.

Kiwi smiled. "Right, let's catch up with him. I don't know how long his bravery will last. I'm worried someone might be leading him into a trap."

They raced to the back of the building just as someone let the door close. "Quick," hissed Kiwi. "Or we'll lose him."

Scampering over, she stuck out her paw and stopped the door. Inside, the lights were out, so cat vision came in very handy. The passageway looked familiar – they had been through it previously, when running from the cellar. In the distance they could hear the sound of pawsteps. The group slunk against the cold, stone wall and tiptoed on their pads along the corridor until they came to the end. Amy and James held their breath all the way.

From around the corner came the rattle of the lift coming down and someone opening the doors. Then they closed and there was a whooshing sound as the lift sped back up. The trio raced around the corner and stared up at the numbers blinking above the lift doors.

"One, two – he's stopped at level two," said Kiwi, pointing to the numbers. The button on the outside of the lift had a lock, but someone had forgotten to remove the key.

"We were on level one when Mr Dogg showed us around, weren't we?" asked James.

"Yes, but now we're going up to level two, which Mr Dogg said was the owner's private residence," said Kiwi.

They waited for what seemed an eternity until the lift reappeared. Kiwi opened the doors and they jumped inside. She pressed the button for level two, noticing there were actually three floors and the cellar. "Here goes…"

Chapter 18: The great escape

The lift whizzed upwards. "What if someone is waiting for us when the lift stops?" asked Amy, shivering slightly.

"Don't worry," said Kiwi. "Furrball knows we are here."

The lift slammed to a stop and the cats all stumbled to their four paws. The door creaked. Kiwi put her ear to it. "I can't hear anyone. Shall we get out?"

The kittens nodded... very slowly. Kiwi pushed the door open with her nose. It squeaked slightly and she poked her whiskers out. The air was cool and the area was dingily lit. She peered around the door. There was nobody in sight and she imagined no-one ever came here, because it looked as if no-one had cleaned it for years. Amy sneezed as her dust allergy kicked in.

Kiwi stepped out of the lift and into the grime-covered room. Cobwebs trailed down from the ceiling, and the wallpaper, blackened with age, hung off the walls in strips. There was no carpet covering the old floorboards, which creaked. "I think it's safe," she said, looking back at the kittens.

Amy and James tiptoed out, closing the lift door quietly. There were not any bulbs in the room, but a blue haze of light spilled in through the window from a streetlight outside. The pane of glass was cracked and a spider idly spun its web in the corner.

"Ugh!"

"What's wrong?" asked Kiwi.

Amy pointed with her nose. "Spiders – they give me the creeps."

"Chicken!" said James.

"I can eat it if you want," suggested Kiwi.

"Nooooo, that's okay. Please don't," mumbled Amy, trembling. "I just won't look at it."

James giggled.

Amy glanced around. "This is spooky and my nose is cold."

"I think we're in a very old part of the building," said Kiwi.

James grinned. "As old as those creepy paintings of men with big moustaches." He sniffed around, as if it was the most natural thing in the world to do when exploring somewhere new.

From nearby came the drip, drip, drip of water, and as the group walked along, the room seemed to creak with a life of its own. The walls appeared to be moving, but it was probably a trick of the light. Ahead there was a mouldy, wooden door with cracks in its panelling. Kiwi bounded over and pushed it open. Beyond was a short landing and a staircase. The three cats made their way up quietly. At the top was another wooden door, this one with an iron knob. Kiwi pushed it slowly and it opened with an eerie sigh.

"Ah!" Amy mewed as a dusty cobweb flew into her face and stuck to her whiskers. She shook her head and wiped her nose with a paw in a bid to remove it.

The door swung back and Kiwi padded into the room beyond. Inside was a row of cabinets, a chair and a small, locked safe. A computer sat to one side on a desk. It was turned off and unplugged. Kiwi tried the cabinets, but they were all locked as well. She glanced around the windowless room. There was nothing else of interest, except for a grey door and an old painting of a dreary landscape. Suddenly, the sound of voices broke the silence.

"Quick! Hide!" hissed Kiwi.

"Where?" mewed Amy.

"Anywhere!"

The door opened and someone came in. The three cats covered their mouths with their paws as the mysterious someone padded across the floor-boards and stopped. Another four paws followed and stopped.

"I thought I heard something," said a voice.

"You're imagining it," said another. "No-one can get up here."

"It must have been a rat or something."

"Or nothing at all. Come on, we've wasted enough time today," hissed the other cat. "We must not fail Dev."

The door closed and all was quiet again. In the distance, the two voices gradually drifted away.

"Phew, that was close," breathed Amy from behind the cabinets.

Kiwi and James poked their noses out from under the desk.

"That was Paws, wasn't it?" asked James softly. "I recognised his voice."

"Yes," said Kiwi, frowning. Furrball was not going to be happy. "I'll buzz the inspector again to let him know we're still here, and then I think we are going to open that grey door."

Amy and James looked at the door, which seemed to loom larger and larger in their imaginations. What was behind it?

After a couple of minutes of pacing, Kiwi listened quietly at the door. Hearing nothing, she pushed it. The door yawned open and they walked into a small room that was completely empty, except for a few boring items of furniture.

"That's odd," remarked Kiwi. "Why were they in this room? There's nothing here."

There were no other doors or any windows; nothing except for a chest of drawers, an old rug and a map of Cat City on the wall. It was a new map, which seemed strangely out of place. The room itself was old and dirty with peeling, blackened wallpaper and cobwebs. A single bulb lit the room with an eerie yellow glow.

Kiwi stalked around. "There must be something in here. Why would anyone come in?"

The kittens paced the room, copying their friend's investigatory actions. They lifted the dusty rug and opened the chest of drawers. They even moved it to see if there was anything behind, but there was nothing. After a while they all sat down in the middle of the room and flicked their tails. Bewildered, they glanced around, and at each other, and around again. Nothing unusual... except... Kiwi's eyes kept darting back to the map – what were Paws and the other catizen looking at on it?

Suddenly, she jumped up. They were not looking AT the map. Of course! She started unpinning it from the wall. "I'm so dumb!" she mumbled, rolling up the map and placing it on the floor.

The three friends stared at the hole in the wall. It was the size of two cats and about a metre off the ground, and it was very dark inside.

"Can you see in there?" asked Amy.

"Not without going in," Kiwi replied.

"That's what I was afraid of."

Kiwi leapt up into the hole and padded into the darkness. It was a tunnel. The air felt cold against her nose and it was pitch black, but she could smell the scent of cats, one of which was Paws. Amy and James took a running jump up behind Kiwi, who kept going. The tunnel went further than she imagined it would, but it didn't narrow.

"Ouch," she hissed, as the ground gave way beneath her feet and she fell… on to floorboards.

"Ouch," hissed the kittens, plunging on top of Kiwi.

"Ooof!" The black cat shook her head from side to side.

"Who are they?" asked James.

A row of scared-looking eyes stared back. The six catizens were seated on the floor, their mouths gagged to prevent them mewing and their paws tied in front of them with rope. The small, dark room was lit by one melting candle. Immediately, they tried to meow through their gags. They were very afraid, except for one, who looked excited and began to wriggle.

"Don't be alarmed," Kiwi whispered. "We're here to save you, but you must help us by being very quiet." Flicking out her claw, she cut the gag on the excited-looking cat and sliced the rope binding his paws.

Released, he cried out, "Am I glad to see you, Kiwi!"

"I'm glad to see you, too, Kip. I was kitty worried."

Kip started purring. The kittens smiled and sprung into action, removing the gags on the other cats and helping to cut the ropes.

"Thank you. I'm Jeremy Katz," said the second cat to be set free.

"We were wondering what became of you all," said Kiwi, taking a look at the gap in the wall. "We need to hurry and get out of here before anyone comes back. Do you know those two catizens who were here before us?"

"They've gone for the night," said Mr Katz, who seemed to be the leader of the group. "They came to feed us. This is where they put us for the night. In the mornings we have to work and they won't come back until then."

"Okay. Is it always the same two catizens who bring you here?" asked Kiwi.

"No, there was one today whom I've never seen before."

"Which one?"

Mr Katz rubbed his head. "The brown one, quite young and a bit podgy around the belly. He was carrying a box."

"Paws!" said James.

"He's working undercover and found you," said Kiwi. "I don't know how. I guess he was going to go back to tell his uncle."

"The other catizen was bigger and ginger with a torn ear," said Mr Katz.

James trembled, remembering the bouncer tomcat and hoping he was far away.

"Right, we'd better get going," said Kiwi. "Is that the only way out?"

"I guess so," said Mr Katz. "I'm afraid we won't be much help because we were always blindfolded when we were brought here."

"Right, everyone follow me. Be very quiet and cross your paws that we'll get out of here in one piece. I'll buzz Furrball that we're coming out and for him to stand by with a van a couple of streets away. We need to leave unnoticed," whispered Kiwi.

Kip purred, thankful to be rescued at last.

Chapter 19: Great work

Inspector Furrball was feeling very proud indeed. "That was great work by Paws. I have to say I'm really surprised. Maybe he'll make a detective yet!"

"Where is the young scamp?" asked Kiwi.

"I've given him the day off," said Furrball. "I think he deserves it. For now the city is happy that all of the catnapped catizens are alive and well, including Kip!"

Kiwi smiled. "Yes, it's kitty good news."

Amy sniffed the wall. "I can hear that scuffling sound again – I think you've still got mice."

"Yes," the inspector sighed. "I think the whole building has them now. If you like, I can train you to catch them!"

Amy went very pale. "Oh, I've already shown them how to be great mouse-catchers," said Kiwi, distracting attention. "Have you spoken to Paws about his new leads?"

"No, not yet," said Furrball. "I'll talk to him tomorrow. I'm quite curious myself."

Kiwi stared out of the window. "When we were in the building we heard voices. We had to hide. One was Paws and the other I didn't recognise. We now know he was talking with the ginger tom – Mr J Catskins' bouncer. He mentioned a catizen called Dev, saying it was important not to let him down. Does the name ring a bell?"

Furrball thought for a second. "No, I can't say it does, but I'll get Siam on to it straight away. I'll buzz Paws and ask him if he knows who this Dev is."

"I was hoping you'd say that," said Kiwi.

Furrball grinned a massive grin. "We are telling everyone that all is well and the catizens are safe. The *Morning Meow* is splashing the good news all over their pages. It might put pressure on the crimicats and bring them out in the open. Perhaps they'll be annoyed and make a mistake now they know they're not going to get the Cat Bills they wanted."

"Should we storm the factory and make arrests?" asked James, rubbing his paws together with glee. "Just like James Bond would."

Furrball frowned. "James who?"

Kiwi waved down the kitten's excitement. "We can't do that. The catizens working there might get hurt or taken hostage. We're also not sure who is involved. As for this Dev, we have to smoke him out, not scare him off."

"The next step is to interview the catnapped catizens," said Furrball, playing with his golden watch chain.

Chapter 20: The catnapped

K iwi carefully poured out nine saucers of fresh, cold lactose-free milk. "Anyone for refreshments?" she asked, without offering the usual brand of biscuits for obvious reasons. Six furry faces nodded and she passed the saucers around.

Amy sat with a pad to take notes, although writing with a paw was rather tricky and she had to bend down several times to retrieve her pencil, which the cat sitting next to her would then try to play with and bat around the floor. She hoped the pencil wouldn't suddenly ping out of her paw and slap some cat between the eyes. Concentrate!

"Right, so how are you all adjusting in the safe house?" asked Kiwi, once the catizens had all settled down and stopped chattering amongst themselves.

"Great."

"Fine."

"Wonderful."

They all nodded to one another.

"It's a relief to be out of that hole," said Kip, toasting the other cats, who responded with a short but hearty burst of applause.

"Good," cheered Kiwi. "We're sorry you can't return to your homes yet, but we think it is safer until we find the catnappers."

"Are our families safe?" asked a black cat with a white nose called Alexander Claws.

"Don't worry, we have a 24-hour Cat Squad guard on your homes and we've increased the number of catsquaddies on the streets," said Kiwi.

"Have you any clues as to who catnapped us?" asked Mr Katz.

"I can't really say, but I was hoping you might have some information that could help us."

All of the cats looked up and Kiwi began her list of questions. There was no slurping from any saucer.

"Did you meet your catnappers?" asked Kiwi.

"Only the two you saw," said Mr Katz. "Sometimes we saw other catizens dressed in black, but they always wore masks to hide their faces."

"Do you know their names?"

"They never mentioned any."

"They were very careful about that," Kip added.

"Can you give a description of the two?" asked Kiwi.

"One was a ginger tom, very big and very crazy, with a torn ear," said Mr Katz.

Kiwi smiled. They knew who he was. The other description the catizens gave fitted Paws, who they saw only once.

"We saw the ginger one most of the time," said Mr Claws.

"When we weren't blindfolded!" chipped in a Persian called Skitkats.

"Eh?" winced a brown cat.

"It was a joke," mumbled Skitkats, having intended to lighten the atmosphere.

"Anyway," continued Mr Katz, "there was also a third catizen who we saw a couple of times. He was a white, short-haired cat with one black paw. He had piercing blue eyes. We saw him on the training days. The ginger one seemed scared of him."

Kiwi was surprised Ginger was frightened of

anyone. "What were the training days?" she asked.

"Well," said Mr Claws, "you see, I'm a builder and Mr Katz is a carpenter, and Skitkats is a plumber – we're all in those sorts of trades."

"Except me, working at Cat Crime," said Kip.

"The white catizen asked us to teach these skills to some of his workers – the ones who make the biscuits. He said he wanted them to have more of an education! We were actually glad he needed us for something and didn't just make us disappear," said Mr Katz.

"Interesting," said Kiwi. "Are they planning to close the factory or build another one? Did you see any plans?"

"Don't know," said Mr Katz. "We didn't see anything like that. We only gave lessons."

Kiwi frowned and glanced at Furrball. If Mr J Catskins intended to build another factory somewhere else, where would he choose? And did it have anything to do with what she had discovered at the bottom of that crate at Cat Crime?

"So, would you know how to make a crate with a false bottom – a secret compartment?" she asked.

Mr Katz looked up. "Yes! Strange you mention it, because I had to show them how to make one. They said it would keep the ingredients of the biscuits secret at the bottom."

"Okay," said Kiwi. "Final questions. How were you treated – honestly?"

"Not too bad," said Kip. "No-one was hurt. It was scary being shut in that room at night and being led around in a blindfold, but no-one harmed us."

"Did they force you to do anything?"

"No," said Mr Claws. "Only to give lessons."

"Well," said Kiwi, standing. "I think that covers everything. I wish you all well and hope to see you all again… under better circumstances when this is all over."

"Meanwhile," added Furrball, "if you think of anything that might help, however unimportant it may seem, do get in touch. And if you have any problems after what you've been through and need someone to talk to, let us know."

Kip smiled. "Hope to see you again soon, Kiwi."

Kiwi grinned back and they nudged heads, purring.

Once the interviewees had filed out of the room, Furrball and Kiwi read through the notes that Amy had made. Afterwards, they went downstairs and passed the description of the white cat – one black paw was unusual – and the name of Dev to Siam, so he could search for the two catizens on his computer.

Chapter 21: Mice?

The following day, Furrball called Kiwi on her catpad to report to Cat Crime. Siam had come up with the goods.

"It seems Dev and the description of the white cat are one and the same," said the inspector once Kiwi and her friends were seated in his office. "Dev is a well-known crimicat. He disappeared from Cat City five years ago, following an arrest for violence, fraud and handling stolen goods. He was described as a white, long-haired cat with one black paw. It seems he has trimmed his fur since and he also has piercing blue eyes. Dev had a reputation for evading the police. His nickname is the Escapologist."

"He's our tom," said Kiwi.

"Are you going to arrest him?" asked Amy.

"For what?" asked Kiwi. "At the moment we have no proof and proof is important, Ames. We've got the catnapped catizens out of the building, but Mr J Catskins may or may not be involved, and Dev could do a runner. No, Dev must be up to something bigger, and we need to find out what it is. Perhaps Paws can tell us something."

Furrball pulled his whiskers. "He's out on special business, undercover. He's gone to meet Ginger to get some information and will report back this afternoon. He didn't want to involve anyone else because he thought Ginger might get suspicious.

"Sounds promising. He's improving."

"So, what can we do?" asked James.

"I think we'll have to wait for Paws," said Furrball.

Kiwi stared up at the map on the wall. Cat City loomed larger and larger. What could Dev's plans be? Why was Mr J Catskins working with him, or was he? Perhaps he knew nothing. And why go to the lengths of catnapping catizens? Why not just hire someone to train the workers? Surely that meant Mr J Catskins knew nothing. There must be something very big happening right under their noses….

"I'm worried how this might end, and there is something important I need to tell you about Dev," said Furrball. "It involves his past and your family…

Kiwi was lost for words. What could it be?

"Ah, not again," moaned the inspector. "That awful scratching – it just gets louder!" He buzzed his secretary. "Miss Kitty, could you set up some more mouse traps please. Try downstairs."

Amy looked up. "You've still got mice?"

"They must be super mice," joked James. He meowed close to the wall. The scratching stopped immediately.

Amy giggled. "Not so super then."

Kiwi and the kittens relaxed and drank some milk, but the scratching soon started again.

James thumped the wall with his paw. "Go away! Run for your little lives!"

Kiwi cocked her head. "Did you hear that?"

"What?" asked Furrball. "Have I got woodworm as well as mice?"

"No, but you might have something worse!" Jumping up, Kiwi smashed the glass containing a little red axe for use in fire emergencies only and gripped it firmly between her paws.

"What are you doing?" shouted Furrball, running out from behind his desk. "Put that down! Have you gone quite mad?"

"Stand back," shouted Kiwi, swinging the axe.

The kittens ran under the desk.

"Nooo!" shouted Furrball, bounding across the room in what seemed slow motion as Kiwi smashed the axe into the wall. "My beautiful wall! Stop! We just decorated!"

Kiwi ignored the inspector and swung the axe again as shards of red-painted wood flew across the room and dust recoloured the carpet. Amy and James cowered beneath the desk. Kiwi swung the axe several more times as the wood creaked, groaned and cracked. Furrball stood still in shock.

"Look!" said Kiwi. "I thought it sounded hollow!"

The cats gathered around and peered into the hole that Kiwi had made. The wall was of very thin wood, painted red, but inside was another wall – the original wall – and in between the two was a cavity.

"What the…?" gasped Furrball.

"Very big mice," Amy remarked.

"It's a room within a room," said James, jumping into the cavity. "Hey, Kiwi, this space runs all the way along the room and keeps going."

"Oh my," sighed Furrball as reality sank in.

"I think we need backup," said Kiwi calmly. "And I think we need it fast before anyone knows we've found their little hidey-hole. Someone has been spying on you, Inspector."

"Right," said Furrball, hitting the red button on his catpad. "Get the Cat Squad ready. Send one squad up now, and get ten more booted and suited. Kiwi, I will have to tell you what I know about Dev another time."

Chapter 22: The maze

K iwi peered into the room within a room. "I think it's safe to say that someone has been listening to everything you say, and who knows where that passage leads? The question is, how long have they been listening?"

The black cat paced up and down, and then rested on the wooden butt of the axe. A gleam flickered across her eyes. "I've got it! The decorators! The mouse noises only started after they had gone."

"Oh no," sighed Furrball. "They painted the entire building." He sat down with a thump.

"But not the outside," said Kiwi. "The catnapped catizens – one is a carpenter, one is a builder, one is a painter… and Dev, well, he's the Escapologist! And those crates had false bottoms. Kip used to work here at Cat Crime. It's all making sense. Where's the catizen who replaced Kip?"

"He's on sick leave," said Furrball, before sitting down again. "Oh no…"

At that moment the door flew open and ten cats burst in, all dressed in red bullet-proof vests, helmets, gloves and boots.

"Whoa!" James exclaimed.

Amy thought they looked very cool. "Their helmets have cat ears!" she whispered to her brother.

"Right," said Furrball, pulling himself together. He grabbed the pistol from his desk drawer and put on a bullet-proof vest under his waistcoat. Then he checked the time on his golden watch. "This is Cat Squad One. Do you want to come with us?"

"Where?" asked Amy.

"Through there," he said, pointing to the hole in the wall. "But I meant Kiwi. It's too dangerous for you."

The kittens nodded, unsure whether to feel relieved or disappointed.

"Miss Kitty will take good care of you," Furrball added. "Two of my agents will mount guard here and the rest of the building is on red alert. No-one leaves and no-one comes in."

"How can you be sure?" asked James.

Furrball smiled. "This is a very special building, Jimster. One day I will explain why, but this is not the time. Right now there is no time to lose." He passed Kiwi a red, protective vest. "I suggest you put this on."

"Good idea," said Kiwi, jumping into the space between the walls. "See you soon, Ames and Jimster. Be good!"

"Be careful," they called out and then looked at one another with serious expressions. Would they see her again? How would they get home if she didn't return? What would their mother say if they appeared without her?

Two of the catsquaddies pushed past Kiwi in the passageway. "Let them go first," said Furrball, raising an eyebrow. Kiwi grinned.

The two catsquaddies walked down the dark passageway, lit by the blue lights on their helmets. They were in a very narrow space, the width of one average-sized cat. It smelt of freshly cut wood and paint due to the lack of fresh air. Another cat had been there recently – they could smell him –

definitely male. It was quite stuffy. Kiwi carried the red axe, which glinted in the blue light, while Furrball had his pistol. "Any idea where we are?" she asked.

"We could knock in a wall to check," suggested Furrball. "Don't worry, Kiwi, I won't bill you for the damage!"

He called forward, the catsquaddies stopped, and Kiwi smashed the axe into the wooden panel. It creaked and splintered, and cracked until a small hole appeared, which they all peered through. "That's a storage room," said Furrball.

They carried on walking. Breathing was a little difficult as there wasn't much air at all and it was very warm. It was also claustrophobic; the wooden walls seemed about to close in at any moment. The group continued on their way until the passage turned a corner. Furrball guessed they were by the library. Kiwi swung the axe. He was right.

They wandered onwards, their pace very slow in the cramped space, pausing now and then to check where they were by making a hole in the wood. After a while, they came to a ladder leading downwards into darkness. The catsquaddie at the front climbed down, undaunted. Kiwi and Furrball squinted in the dark until they could see him. He gave the thumbs-up and they climbed down.

"We're on the second floor," said Furrball.

They crept along, checking their location every now and then. Past the canteen, toilets, the investigative room, pressroom and the research room.

"They've been listening to everything," Furrball sighed.

"Even when you were on the cat litter," joked Kiwi.

"Glad you find it funny."

"Sometimes you have to laugh when something goes wrong that you can't help," she whispered.

Suddenly they heard something or someone move around the next corner. The cats stopped dead in their tracks and listened to the silence. The sound emerged again and it was not far away. The catsquaddie in front gave the signal to wait while he ran bravely around the corner with his gun at the ready. The rest of the group waited with baited breath for the all-clear. In no time at all, he ran back and gave the thumbs-up – there was no-one there.

"Maybe they heard us," said Furrball.

"Maybe not," whispered Kiwi. "The sound could have carried from another room."

"By the way, I've sent two teams to stake out Mr J Catskins' factory," said Furrball. "No-one will be able to leave that fishy place."

"Kitty good thinking."

They walked a little further and then Kiwi created another hole to see where they were.

"Oh no," exclaimed Furrball. "It's the interview room. Everything has been overheard."

"Looking on the bright side, it's a good thing we put the catizens in a safe house," said Kiwi.

Furrball nodded and the group pressed on, around the next bend, until they came to another ladder. The first catsquaddie climbed down it while the others waited.

"I didn't realise you had the entire building redecorated," said Kiwi.

"Yes, the mayor gave us a bigger budget this year."

Soon, the catsquaddie reappeared and gave the thumbs-up. "It leads to the ground floor," he said.

"There's one place we didn't decorate – the delivery bay down there," Furrball told Kiwi as he crept down the ladder.

Once again, the cats were in a wooden corridor, the floor of which was strewn with woodchips and dust. In the distance they spied a very small cat flap. The first catsquaddie signalled for everyone to step back and silence fell over the group. He walked slowly towards the cat flap and pushed it. There was a sudden bang and he slumped to the floor.

"Everyone get back!" meowed Furrball.

The second catsquaddie checked the settings on his gun and blasted the cat flap with a stream of ice. It disintegrated in a cloud of white dust. "He's alive," he called out. "It's just a superficial wound."

In the distance someone could be heard running away. When the icy dust from the blast cleared, the cats found themselves in an empty room with two exits. There was also a smashed computer, a chair and a radio. Kiwi stopped, opened her collar and gave the injured catsquaddie a special purple tablet to swallow, while Furrball called for assistance on his catpad.

"Better call for another squad while you're at it," said Kiwi. "Who knows what lies ahead?"

"Which direction, sir?" asked the second catsquaddie, who now had the lonesome task of going first.

"Take your pick," said Furrball. "I think this was designed to confuse and delay us." He then turned to the injured tomcat, sad to leave him behind on his own, and told him, "Another squad is coming right now – you'll be alright."

The second catsquaddie led the group through the right-hand exit and down yet another long passage, constructed of wood. The area was in complete blackness, barely lit by the blue lights on the cats' helmets. They had to rely on their night vision, but, being cats, it was pretty good and, luckily, quite reliable in tricky situations such as these. Suddenly there was a loud clunk and the sound of something sliding. Everyone stopped and looked up at the ceiling. Something was moving – it was behind them.

"Run!" shouted the second catsquaddie.

The cats at the front of the group charged forwards, seconds before a sheet of steel smashed down behind them, sealing off the way they had come and cutting them off from the catsquaddies at the back.

"That was rotten luck," said Furrball. "Backup won't be able to follow us either."

"We should have taken the left exit," said someone.

"Keep going," said Kiwi, knowing there was no use crying over spilt milk, as the saying goes. "What's done is done."

The second catsquaddie stormed ahead and the others chased his tail. The corridor turned and turned, and then stopped abruptly. The wood ended and a dirty, stone tunnel continued.

"I think we're in the sewage system," said someone.

"Do you know where?" asked another.

"It whiffs a bit," said a third voice.

Kiwi checked her compass. "We're heading east."

"Catskins' factory is in the east," said Furrball. "Let's see where this takes us."

After half an hour of walking in a straight line, the cats came to the end of the stone tunnel, which stopped at a ladder, leading up to a manhole shaped like a cat's head. The second squaddie grimaced and made his way up the ladder, with his gun slung over his shoulder. Two other squaddies moved to the bottom of the ladder and aimed their firearms at the manhole. The other cats took up positions further back. They all waited.

When the second catsquaddie reached the top of the ladder, he stretched up his paws and heaved the manhole cover upwards and across ever so slowly. Down below, everyone looked up in trepidation. A shaft of orangey light flooded down the ladder and illuminated everyone below.

"Am I glad to see you!" a happy voice mewed as a furry face appeared over the hole.

"Oh my, it's Paws!" gasped Furrball.

"Hello, Uncle! Are you alright?"

Chapter 23: The hunt for Dev

The second catsquaddie climbed up the ladder and the rest of the group followed. Soon they were all standing in a round, white room without any furnishings of any kind and with one closed door.

"What are you doing here?" Furrball asked his nephew.

"Waiting for you," said Paws. "I met up with Ginger and was trying to get to a meeting with Dev. I was pretending to be a new recruit. One of Dev's gang came running out of this hole, saying he was being followed by the Cat Squad. I said I would keep watch and he went to find Dev. They're up to something big, but I think they've had to change their plans – you may have messed them up a bit."

Kiwi laughed. "I hope so."

"What were you doing in the sewer?" asked Paws.

"It's a long story," said Furrball. "I'll tell you later. Do you know where Dev is now?"

"I don't," groaned Paws. "I guess he's with Ginger and Mr J Catskins. Have you called for backup? We need it. How will we get out of here?"

"We can escape through the sewage system if we have to," butt in Kiwi.

"If the other squad can get through that steel door," Furrball sighed.

Paws frowned, looking confused.

"Come on, catizens," said Furrball. "This isn't over until the fat cat sings."

Kiwi looked straight at Paws who blushed.

The second catsquaddie checked his gun and took up his position at the front of the group. He opened the door of the room and checked outside: all clear. The others followed him out.

"Where are we exactly?" said Kiwi, voicing the question everyone seemed to have forgotten to ask.

"In an old part of the Catskins factory, in the basement," Paws replied. "If we go that way, we'll get to the cellar. We could leave that way or take the lift. It goes to levels one, two and three – the roof."

"Okay, let's take the lift," said Furrball.

The second catsquaddie led the way. The group squeezed inside the lift and Paws pressed the button for level one. It shook, whizzed up and stopped all of a sudden. The catizens wobbled to their paws. Four catsquaddies aimed their catguns at the doors as they creaked and opened. The warehouse beyond was empty. Kiwi recognised it. The second catsquaddie charged out in front and paced swiftly around the warehouse, checking to make sure no-one was hiding in the corners.

Furrball and Kiwi stood quietly to one side with Paws. Behind them, the five other catsquaddies waited. "All clear," said the second squaddie. The cool air made Kiwi's whiskers bristle. She felt nervous for some reason.

"We should go that way," said Paws, pointing. "It leads to the manufacturing area and…"

"Drop your weapons!"

Stunned, Kiwi jumped. The voice came from above.

"W-what the…?" stammered Furrball as the catsquaddies aimed their guns towards the rafters.

Three figures stood on the metal walkway above their heads, aiming guns back at them. Kiwi could make out Ginger, a white cat and a brown cat who looked familiar – Mr Dogg!

"I said drop your weapons!" hissed the white cat with one black paw.

Kiwi pounced on Furrball and pushed him to the ground as the catsquaddies opened fire on the metal walkway above. The shots of pure ice ricocheted noisily off the metal beam with electrifying echoes. Just then there came a banging sound from behind them and a creaking crash as a grey cloud of soot filled one side of the warehouse. The cats coughed and spluttered. Kiwi wiped her eyes. Through the smoke, she could see rows of black-booted paws and their guns were aimed at the catsquaddies.

"Another fake wall," Kiwi sighed. "We were so naive to come walking in here." They were surrounded.

"What now?" asked Furrball.

"I think we better do as they say," said Paws, getting up from the floor. "You have no choice. Drop your weapons and remove your catpads."

"He said you, not we," said Furrball in shock.

Paws backed away towards the row of black-clad cats, brushing the soot off his paws. Kiwi and the inspector stared at him in disbelief.

"So that's why he was in that room where we found the six catnapped catizens," said Kiwi as everything clicked into place in her mind.

"You didn't expect me to have no ambition, did you, Uncle?" asked Paws. "I wasn't quite the bungling little idiot you took me for."

Inspector Furrball threw his pistol across the floor. "Catsquaddies, drop your catguns."

"Take them to the white room," shouted the white cat with the piercing blue eyes as he crossed the high metal beam.

"Drop your catguns and catpads in a pile over there," meowed Paws, kicking the weapons in that direction. "We don't want anyone getting any funny ideas or attempting any heroics."

The catizens disarmed, and removed their catpads and protective clothing. Paws allowed his uncle to keep his waistcoat with the little gold watch chain on it – family and all that. The bad cats marched them in single file across the warehouse, through the factory and out of the green door that Kiwi remembered from before. Then Paws unlocked the white door – the room Mr Dogg had not shown them on the day of their visit. They were all marched into a massive, round, white room with a circular table in the centre, surrounded by black cushions.

Paws nodded to the black-clad cats, who clicked their guns menacingly. "Put them in there!" meowed Dev, entering the room and pointing to a steel door at the far end. Paws unlocked it. "We must decide what we're going to do with you," Dev hissed, "now you've put us to so much inconvenience."

"What do you want?" Furrball asked him.

Dev bared his teeth. "Everything!"

The cats in black drew their weapons and waved Furrball, Kiwi and the six catsquaddies into the room. Single-file, they walked in forlornly and the steel door slammed shut behind them. They were in an oblong-shaped, stone room without any windows

– a cell, basically. A non-Cat City bulb shone a depressing, yellow light. Kiwi noticed a row of scratched claw marks along the wall. Someone had been counting the days and weeks for some time. In the far corner, a shadow moved in the dim light. Kiwi moved closer. Something was there, under a large, dark-coloured blanket. It gave off a low, meowing sound.

"Hello?" she whispered, edging closer still. "We're not going to hurt you."

The mewing continued. On the floor by the heap sat an empty saucer and a half-eaten bowl of food.

"Are you alright?" Kiwi asked, sniffing whoever it was. Her whiskers bristled as the body beneath trembled. Carefully, she nudged the blanket with her nose and pulled it back with her teeth.

"Madame Purrfect!" exclaimed Inspector Furrball, throwing his paws up in the air. Stunned, he stood with his mouth wide open. "What on earth are you doing here?"

"Roger?" stammered the softly spoken Burmese.

"Yes, it's me," he said. "Are you alright? You look very pale. What are you doing here? How long have…?"

Kiwi glanced once more at the claw marks on the wall.

"A very long time," said Madame Purrfect, sniffing away her tears. "Since Mr J Catskins took over the factory."

"Oh no," Furrball cried out, "surely not?! That was a year ago. I thought you had gone on a cruise. Then we heard you had gone to stay with relatives by the sea after selling the factory."

"Complete cat litter," said Madame Purrfect, getting to her paws. "I've been locked in here. I'm only alive because Dev's father wouldn't let anything bad happen to me. Otherwise, who knows where I'd be? Dev is evil and he'll stop at nothing to get what he wants."

"You mentioned Dev's father?" asked Kiwi.

"Mr J Catskins is his father," explained Madame Purrfect. "He wanted him to finally come home and he has."

Furrball gave his long-lost friend a huge hug. "Dev has put a lot of effort into planning all this. He infiltrated Cat Crime and maybe he has done the same elsewhere, such as the mayor's office?"

"With knowledge like that he could take over Cat City," said Kiwi. "But perhaps all is not lost. We should whisper – we don't know if the walls here have ears too." She wondered what Furrball had wanted to tell her about Dev's past.

Chapter 24: The catsurveillance team

Outside Catskins, hidden among the trees, six vans of catsquaddies stood guard. No-one had tried to enter or leave the building, according to the catsurveillance team in the back of one of the vans. Back at Cat Crime, everyone was still on red alert – the secret passageways were being guarded and any new biscuit deliveries across the city were being searched (but not eaten). Other squaddies combed the sewage system, trying hard not to sniff anything while seeking another way into the Catskins factory.

"What's happening?" asked Amy, huddled with James in the back of the catsurveillance van. "We haven't heard from Furrball or Kiwi in ages."

Chip, an expert at spying, removed his headphones. "Don't worry, Ames. We are the ears and eyes of the outfit, and we're not going to miss anything. It's up to the tough cats and Detective Siam to decide when to go in – if at all. We have catsquaddies in the sewers below the factory; you can follow them here on this camera. They all have special cameras in their helmets and carry radios, and they are reading to go in and help if needed."

"Wow," said James, "very James Bond."

"James who?" asked Chip. Shrugging, he put his headphones back on.

Just then the van doors flew open and Siam leapt in. The kittens greeted him, and asked if there was any news on Furrball and Kiwi.

"No," said Siam, "but we could use your help."

Amy and James were astonished. How could they possibly be of help? They were too young and small.

Siam sat down and looked at them gravely. "We haven't had any contact from our friends for quite a while, since they came out of the sewers. They could be anywhere in that building. We don't have a blueprint of the inside whereas you two…"

"…have been inside," Amy said, completing his sentence.

"Exactly, Ames. We have agents waiting, but we don't know where to send them. They don't want to walk into an ambush."

"We never went into the sewers," said James. "I don't know where they would come up."

"What's the lowest level in the building?" asked Siam.

"The cellar," Amy replied.

"Okay, so there is a possibility they will come up there," said Siam.

"There are two exits from the cellar and one leads outside," she remembered. "There's a lift there, so they should take that. It goes to levels one, two and three – the roof."

James joined in: "Level two needs a key in the lift and it's really old-looking there, but we found the catnapped catizens in a secret tunnel up there."

Siam scratched his head. "Now I'm confused. What about the main entrance?"

"Uh, when you go in there's a hallway and a staircase going up," said Amy. "You go up and there's a green door, which leads to the warehouse where they make biscuits."

"There's a metal walkway going across it – might

126

be a dodgy place for an ambush," suggested James, not knowing how right he was.

"Okay," said Siam. "Can you two draw me something?"

The kittens grinned and nodded. Using the knowledge they had, they sketched a map of the cellar, levels one and two, and anything else they could remember, although they were not sure how some of it connected up. "We can't draw the roof. We got ejected down a slippery slide!"

Siam looked amazed. "Thanks. I'll get these copied and hand them out."

"There's one other thing," added James. "There is a room with a white door, next to a green door. Mr Dogg didn't show us inside. I think it was locked. Maybe it's important."

Siam made a note before heading off. Twenty cat minutes later, he was back. "We're going in," he announced.

"Can we come?" asked Amy.

"Aha, I guessed you'd ask that. To keep you safe, put on these Cat Squad vests and visors, and these boots," he said. Smiling, he held out mini-versions of his own red outfit. "I'm sending two Cat Squads up to the roof and we're going in the front with three more. Backup is on standby. Our cats in the sewers are going to enter the building at the same time."

"Will we be able to get in the front door?"

"Well, we're definitely not going to ring the bell!" said Siam with a laugh.

Five minutes later, the catsquaddies cut through the front gates, raced up the pathway and entered the main entrance to Mr J Catskins' factory. Up above, other squaddies smashed through the windows of the second floor, abseiling on bright red ropes.

"Wow, this is more exciting than any comic," said James.

"Yeah, but these vests really itch," Amy hissed.

"Ah, my sister has fleas!"

Chapter 25: The hit squad

Siam stormed the building first, flanked by the catsquaddies, while Amy and James trotted along somewhere in the middle of the pack between some very muscular, big tomcats. Siam stopped and turned to look at the kittens. When they nodded, he charged up the emerald-carpeted stairs with everyone else in tow. A tom and a queen stayed by the entrance with their weapons drawn.

The other cats charged to the top of the staircase, heading for the white room. As the first catsquaddie turned the corner, a wave of bullets rang out, and the rest of the cats dove for cover on the stairs. The squaddies leapt, rolled and fired blasts of ice as shots rang out, and two cats guarding the white room fell to the floor, frozen.

"They froze?" asked Amy, unable to believe what she was seeing, but Siam did not hear her. He jumped up and tried the door, which was locked. "Blast it," he instructed and stood back as two cats opened fire. The wood froze into a block of ice and then expanded. Fragments of wood flew out as it blew to smithereens. Voices could be heard above the commotion.

"Wow," gasped James.

"Don't move," shouted the catsquaddies as they moved into the white room. The first thing they saw were three cats sitting on black cushions around a white table.

"That's Mr Dogg," said Amy, pointing, "and he's Mr J Catskins."

"And that one's Ginger," whispered James, doing his hardest not to tremble. The bouncer cat scowled at him.

"Thank kitty, it's you!" mewed a cat, bounding across the room. It was Paws, out of breath and gripping a gun. He was beaming from ear to ear. "I thought you'd never turn up. I haven't heard from Uncle for hours. Have you seen him?"

"No," said Siam, noticing six cats dressed in black. They were standing at the opposite end of the room with their guns pointed at the three cats sitting around the table. "I see you already have the situation under control."

"Only just," said Paws. "We were outnumbered, but managed to defeat their tomcats. We put them in that metal-doored cell behind me, so they can't cause any more harm. I was interrogating these three about Dev."

"You'll never find him," hissed Mr J Catskins. "He'll escape you yet again."

"Silence," said Paws.

"Do you have any information on Dev or his whereabouts?" asked Siam, leaning on the butt of his gun.

"Sort of, but I don't want to tell you in front of them – let's go outside," Paws suggested. Turning to the six cats in black, he nodded at the three suspects and said, "Put them in the cell." The six cats grinned.

"Come on, let's go outside," Siam told the catsquaddies.

Amy and James followed them into the hallway, relieved to be away from Ginger's intimidating stare.

"Let's take the green door," said Paws.

Once they were all inside, Siam closed the door. The cats' boots echoed as they walked across the wooden floor of the manufacturing room. "We can talk here," Paws said. The catsquaddies stopped behind him, and Amy and James scampered up, but Paws kept walking. "Let's go to the warehouse. I have some important information to show you."

"Can't you show us here?" asked Siam.

"It's on a computer in the warehouse," replied the brown cat, turning to face him and stepping backwards.

James noticed something glisten around Paws' neck. Something red that caught the light.

Siam stared around the warehouse. It was quiet. "So what was your lead on Dev? Where is he?"

"We saw him earlier," said Paws, shuffling from side to side, "but he escaped us. We did manage to capture the others though, as you saw."

Siam grimaced. "How did he get away?"

It must be a jewel, thought James. Glass wouldn't catch the light in that way.

Paws sighed. "He had more men with him than we thought. He ambushed us."

"Where?"

"Upstairs. Level two, in the old part of the building. He ran off in the direction of where we found the catnapped catizens. I think there might be some secret passages there, too."

"Secret passages?" asked Siam. He was sure no-one had told Paws about the ones at Cat Crime.

Whatever it was around his neck, it was definitely not gold-plated, thought James. It was real gold, like his mother's necklaces, and it was such an unusual design...

Paws shrugged. "I mean, like the secret tunnel behind the map on level two. It led to the catnapped catizens."

"Ah," Siam sighed, shocked at his own suspicions. Paws was Furrball's nephew after all.

"The only way to level two is to take the lift," said Paws.

"Where is that?"

"It's in the warehouse," said Amy.

Paws looked impatient. "We shouldn't be wasting so much time. Dev could be anywhere. He might have left level two. I could show you the information on the computer in the warehouse on the way..."

"Yes, I see. Sounds a good idea," Siam agreed.

James had stopped walking. Such an unusual design, he thought, staring down at the ground while he concentrated. A fish. A red fish with bones and a tail. Then it hit him all of a sudden in a moment of cold realisation – he had seen that fish before... not so long ago... in the painting... in the hallway! He looked up. Paws and Siam were already heading in the direction of the warehouse.

"The fish," James cried out. "The fish!"

Siam stopped in his tracks and turned as James sprinted towards him, mewing, "The necklace around his neck – it isn't his... it doesn't belong to him!"

The Siamese stopped and glanced at Paws, who looked as if he had just seen a ghost.

"It belongs to Madame Purrfect," James finished.

"M-madame Purrfect?" mumbled Siam, and he

132

turned to Paws whose eyes were darting all over the place. "Let me see it."

"He's talking rubbish," said Paws, angrily. "How could it be? She left Cat City a year ago. I never even met her."

"It's the same as the necklace she's wearing in the painting in the hallway," shouted James. "Siam, you have to believe me!"

Amy stood next to her brother. "I've seen the picture too."

"Is that so?" asked Siam, snatching the pendant from around the neck of Paws, who backed away and started to run. "It seems we've been outfoxed."

"Isn't that out-catted?" asked Amy.

"Outfoxed," repeated Siam, looking confused. "Stop or I'll shoot. I don't care whose nephew you are."

Paws stopped and his head sunk to his furry chest. He threw his gun across the floor, just as pawsteps could be heard running across the warehouse.

"See who that is," shouted Siam and five cat-squaddies charged towards the source of the sound.

"Lay on the floor," shouted Siam. Paws slumped to the ground, covered his head with his paws and wrapped his bushy tail closely around him. "Now, how exactly did you get that necklace?"

Paws said nothing. Soon the catsquaddies ran back. "Sir, someone was in the lift. It went up to level two. Do you want us to follow?" one asked.

"No," said Siam. "Suspects on level two," he spoke into his catpad before turning to Paws. "So you were leading us into a trap? That's nice."

Paws said nothing.

"To think how long I've known you and I even helped with your training," said Siam. He then let out a huge sigh as something else dawned on him. "Catsquaddies, go back to the white room. I hate to think who is really in that cell, but I fear those catizens dressed in black were not on our side."

The catsquaddies, all except two, turned on their heels and sped off.

"I'm arresting you for being a traitor to Cat City," Siam told Paws. "You have the right to remain silent, but anything you meow or purr will be noted. Squaddies, take him to the van and freeze him."

"Freeze him?" asked Amy. "So those cats back there were frozen, but how?"

"Ah, you don't know," said Siam. "Our catguns freeze. You've seen how they fire ice. Well, we freeze suspects and later we de-freeze them!"

"Wow!" gasped James. "Like a big lolly!"

Siam turned his gun on Paws. Amy and James winced as he pulled the trigger and a jet of icy air zoomed out, turning Paws into a block of ice. They could see his dark shadow inside.

"It lasts about two to three hours," said Siam.

"Paws-cubes!" giggled James.

The kittens watched as two catsquaddies picked up the block of Paws and carried him outside to be taken to Cat Crime.

"I can't believe he's a traitor," said Amy.

Siam shook his head. "Nor me. I didn't see that coming. I actually thought he was stupid."

The group raced back to the white room in time to see the cats in black being handcuffed by catsquaddies. "So, you were waiting for Paws to return, were you, after he led us into an ambush?" bellowed Siam. "I think you underestimated us," he added, winking at James.

Ginger sniggered. No-one else said a word.

"Who is in the cell, Catskins?" asked Siam.

Silence.

"Suspect failed to assist," said Siam.

The catsquaddies bundled the suspects into the corner, read them their rights and handcuffed them with little red cuffs.

"Where's the key to this metal door?" Siam asked, but no-one replied. "Will someone blow that cell door!" he said impatiently.

"Everyone inside, get away from the door," a catsquaddie shouted out.

There was a shuffling sound inside the cell as Inspector Furrball and Kiwi pushed the others to the back of the oblong-shaped area, where they crouched down.

The catsquaddie pasted some red plaster around the door. "Everyone, take cover!" he shouted and then ran into the far corner of the room. With a small explosion and a puff of ice fragments, the door spun open on its broken hinges.

"I wondered when you would finally get here!" said Kiwi, her nose poking out of the ice cloud. Amy and James sprinted towards her, purring loudly.

"I'm afraid I have some very bad news for you, sir," said Siam as Furrball emerged from the cell. "It's your nephew, Paws, he…"

"I know," said the inspector gravely. "Guess how we ended up in here?"

Siam was astounded, but it was all starting to

make sense. "So, Paws didn't actually find the catnappers that day?"

"It seems he helped to catnap them," said Furrball. "We tried to warn you when we heard you talking in the room with Paws, but you couldn't hear us."

"No, we couldn't," said Siam. "That was close – we were nearly ambushed."

"But we're all safe now," purred Amy.

"We really need to find Dev," said Kiwi. Her head was almost bursting with all the new information she had learnt from Furrball while they were stuck in the cell.

Siam thought quickly. "I'll call for backup. You two tomcats, freeze these suspects and take them to the van. The rest of you come with us."

"Paws said Dev was on level two," said Amy.

Kiwi frowned. "That would be pointless. The only places worth going would be the exits or the roof."

"All exits are covered," said Siam.

"How about the sewers?"

"Also covered."

"That leaves the roof," said Kiwi.

"Let's go," yelled Siam.

"Well, this is definitely no place for a lady," said Furrball to Madame Purrfect. "I think you should wait here. Our vans are outside and one of my toms can lead you outside safely."

"I don't think so," she replied. "I have a few things I want to say to this Mr Dev myself!"

"Alright!" purred Amy.

"Before we go, Madame Purrfect," said Siam, "I

think this belongs to you." He passed her the fish pendant.

Tears filled the Burmese cat's eyes as she turned it over in her paws. "I thought I would never see this again. Thank you so much."

"Thank Jimster," said Siam. "He noticed it. In fact, if he hadn't noticed it, we would have been ambushed."

Furrball beamed. "Well done, Jimster!"

"Yes, good for you," said Madame Purrfect, rubbing Jimster's nose. "This necklace was a present and it's irreplaceable." She smiled at Furrball, who went very, very red indeed.

With no time to lose, the group of cats raced into the manufacturing area and across the warehouse floor. The rooms were deserted. They charged into the cellar and bundled inside the lift – a tight squeeze – just as the doors closed. The lift vibrated and shuddered as it rose slowly upwards.

"What if they're waiting for us?" asked Amy.

No-one answered – they were all thinking the exact same thing. They waited silently as the lift crept up and up, seeming to take forever, until it ground to an unsteady, sudden stop. Every cat stumbled, collapsed and got up again. The door squeaked open.

One of the catsquaddies poked his nose out while everyone else held their breath. "All clear," he said.

The cats sighed with relief and padded out, one by one. They were in a corridor, lit by a yellow light, with one door at the end. Kiwi charged over to it and threw it open. She's so brave, thought Siam, hurrying to keep up with her. Stone steps crept up to another door. Kiwi led the way, but Siam politely pushed past her and kicked the door open. A breeze chilled his nose. He was on the roof. The air whistled past his ears and made his whiskers bristle.

The cats moved out and stared around the empty space, hemmed in by a wire fence. Several injured catsquaddies lay on the ground, along with some cats in black, frozen into cubes.

"They must have been ambushed here," said Siam.

One of the injured squaddies looked up and cried out, "Duck!" just before a shot rang out across the rooftop.

"Everyone, hide!" meowed Kiwi.

Some of the group took cover behind some crates while the catsquaddies darted forth and blasted ice at some black-clad cats who charged out of hiding, shooting bullets. Amy covered her ears with her paws.

"Don't move," said Kiwi to the kittens. "Sorry to put you in danger."

"Don't move," mimicked a cat in a black waistcoat gripping a rifle. "Don't move as much as a whisker, little kitties!"

Kiwi, Amy and James froze.

"Don't you move either!" came a shout as the black cat fell stunned to the ground. Madame Purrfect clapped her paws together to the amazement of all the others. Kiwi turned her gun on the unconscious tomcat and froze him. Zap!

"Glad to see those self-defence lessons didn't go to waste, Madame Purrfect," said Inspector Furrball, dashing past with his pistol at the ready. "Take that, you slime cats!"

Kiwi got up, hearing a faint, whizzing sound. Looking around, she couldn't see what it could be, but it was coming from the far end of the roof. She bounded towards the edge and balanced on a ledge in front of a wall. Siam noticed and raced after her. In the distance on the next roof, which was higher than the one Kiwi stood on, was a caticopter and it was about to take off. She could see a cat sitting in the pilot seat and she guessed it was Dev.

"Over there!" she meowed as Siam and several catsquaddies caught up with her. "Dev is getting away!"

Together, the cats scaled the wall in front of them using their sharp claws and leapt across the gap between the two rooftops, landing with a thud as the blades of the caticopter whirred. It was perched on a high ledge. One of the squaddies opened fire with his freeze gun, but he was too far away.

"Stop him!" yelled Furrball, watching from the roof of Catskins' factory.

Kiwi gritted her teeth and decided to go for the longest jump she had ever attempted. Arching her back, she made a leap for the ledge on which the caticopter still sat. She sailed through the air, further and further, higher and higher, using her tail to balance. As she closed in on the caticopter, the air from the whizzing blades pushed against her body. It whooshed past her ears and flattened her whiskers. Trying with all her might, she landed with a thud on the ledge, but she was too late. The caticopter lifted off.

"No!" mewed Kiwi. Through the pilot's glass window, she could just make out Dev's piercing, laughing blue eyes as he made his escape from the rooftop, up into the clouds, away from Cat City.

"Did you see that?" gasped the impressed kittens, secretly hoping that one day in the far distant future, if they trained hard enough, they might be able to copy such a jump. Siam nodded.

"We were so close!" sighed Kiwi, her tail drooping. There were so many questions she had wanted to ask him about the past.

"I'm afraid that's why they call him the Escapologist," said Furrball, slapping Kiwi on the back. "Don't worry, he's no longer a threat to us – at least for now – and we arrested Mr Dogg, Catskins and Ginger, and all their crimicats. Not to mention my troublesome nephew. On top of that, we rescued the delightful Madame Purrfect."

At the mention of her name, the Burmese catizen smiled warmly. "Thank you again!"

"And we're all safe and sound," quipped Amy.

"So it was a good day then," said James.

"I guess you can't have everything all of the time," admitted Kiwi with a smile. "But, I have a feeling we haven't seen the last of Dev."

"There's just one thing I was wondering," said Amy.

"What's that?" asked Kiwi.

"What was in the bottom of that crate you found at Cat Crime?"

"That, my little Ames is another story for another day," said Furrball. "Now, who fancies some nice milk and biscuits, but not the Catskins kind?"

The kittens clapped their paws together and purred.

The End of the Tail
Or is it?
Keep reading for a sneak peak at
Kiwi and the Missing Magic…

Kiwi and the Missing Magic

Chapter 1: Home again, home again

"Okay, kids, I think it's time I took you home!"

"Ohhhhhh," sighed Amy and James. "Do we have to?"

"I'm afraid so," mewed Kiwi, running ahead. "Come on! You know the drill! We have to quickly say goodbye to Georgy, race down the tunnel and head across the field to the bluebells. Remember? And don't forget to prepare for the landing. It can be a bit hard!"

"Okay," the kittens mewed, chasing after the speedy feline.

With Kiwi in front they raced across the field towards the clump of bluebells. Suddenly, the black cat vanished in a puff of purple smoke. The kittens followed. A shimmer of light surrounded them, like a bubble being blown from washing-up liquid, except it was purple and glowing. The bubble enlarged until it suddenly popped.

The field vanished and the kittens were falling, down, down, down. Purple smoke whooshed all around them as they fell, twisting and turning, their tails turned up between their legs. They had the weird sensation of falling through endless space. It was a much different feeling than on the journey to Cat City.

They landed with a thud in the field. The grass felt damp and the air was cold. It was dark. Amy checked her watch: 4am. They had only been gone for a couple of hours!

"Ouch!" James rubbed his feet, which were no longer fluffy paws. "It's dark. Is it still the same night?"

"I think so," replied Amy. "My watch says 4am."

"Wow," said James, wiping his forehead.

"I know. What a day... or night... or week," said Amy. "I'm a bit stunned."

"Me too, it's a bit weird being home."

"It's cold," added Amy, hugging herself.

"That's because you don't have any fur," laughed James.

"Ha ha!" said Amy. "You were a less annoying brother as a cat. Or rather kitten. You were so tiny!"

"Come on you two!" squeaked Kiwi, staring at them with that look she had, as if immense time was being wasted. "Got to get you both home and into bed before your parents wake up."

"Ah, mum and dad," stuttered James.

"What do we tell them?" asked Amy.

"They're not going to believe it," sighed James.

"No way! Not at all. It's too crazy," said Amy. "Unless they come and see for themselves."

"Wait 'til I tell Dan. He's going to go wild..."

"And Jeanie..."

"NO!" snarled Kiwi.

Amy and James jumped.

Kiwi wagged her tail and her eyes glared. "You cannot tell anyone. ANYONE. No-one must know about this. EVER."

Amy and James gulped. Kiwi had never looked so scary. They were glad they weren't mouse shaped.

143

The little black cat sat down. "Sorry, I didn't want to scare you, but it's a secret. You can't tell anyone."

"But why?" asked James.

"Mum would be so happy to be able to talk to you. Remember all those times she had to take you to the vet? This way you could tell her what's wrong rather than the vet guessing. Remember all those worming tablets and how they turned out to be a waste of time?"

"Yes," replied Kiwi, shivering at the memory. Whoever invented those must have wanted to create the worst tasting thing in the universe. "Please don't mention the worming tablets..."

James giggled. "Mum had to tickle you to get you to open your mouth, and then she just hid them in your food..."

"Yes, yes," said Kiwi, embarrassed. "Very funny! Now, back to the point... you can't tell anyone because first of all no-one will believe you. If people do believe you, then they will want proof, and then people will be watching us all of the time. Your parents would be worried. People who believed the story would demand to go to Cat City. And I would be in trouble in Cat City for taking you there in the first place. They all think you're cats! Then what would I do? I would have to leave both of my homes."

"Nooooo," cried James.

"Yes," nodded Kiwi. "I like being anonymous. I like people thinking I'm just a normal cat. Imagine all of the questions. The police might take me away for questioning..."

"Okay," said Amy. "We won't tell anyone. It's a shame though. I wish everyone could talk to you."

"Well, some do," said Kiwi. "You know, animals, insects – just not humans, except you two."

"Wow – can we talk to other animals?" they both asked.

Kiwi wondered. "I'm not sure. You just have to listen in the right way. You have to know when to listen."

"When's that?" asked James.

"When you're not asking questions!" laughed Amy, nudging him. He poked her back.

By this time they had reached the back gate of their garden and they crept inside. The back door of the house was still unlocked, so they sneaked inside. Kiwi padded to her bed by the settee in the lounge, and Amy and James tiptoed upstairs. What an adventure. Wow! They both yawned as they got ready for bed in their separate rooms, thinking their own separate thoughts. They had gone on an adventure with their pet cat! Their talking pet cat in a land full of talking cats!

Unknown to one another, the children both looked out of their bedroom windows into the dark night sky and up at the silvery moon, which continued to glow brightly, shaped weirdly like a cat's claw. In both of their minds there was just one thought: how soon would they be going back to Cat City?!

Chapter 2: Back to school

"James, can you stop slurping your milk? Just because I've got my back turned doesn't mean that I don't know what you're doing!" said mother.

Oh no! James quickly stopped lapping the milk from his bowl of cereal and sat up straight. How did that happen? One minute he was eating his cornflakes with a spoon and the next minute he had his head in the bowl, licking up the milk... like a cat. There was milk all over the table and he hadn't even realised he was doing it.

Amy had her hand clasped over her mouth, trying not to explode into laughter. Her eyes were popping and her body wiggled. On the other chair, Kiwi had her paws over her head, also trying not to break into giggles. She purred softly.

Concentrating, James spooned the cornflakes into his mouth, frowning at his sister.

"So, are you two ready for school after the long weekend?" asked Mother.

"Eh, not really," said Amy. "I've got that maths test today."

"You'll do well," said mother. "You studied hard."

"Yeah, but I just couldn't sleep!" said Amy.

James winked. Their mum finished making her coffee and sat down at the table, her hands warming on the mug. "What about you, James? Cat got your tongue?"

That was too much! Amy exploded into laughter, James coughed on his cornflakes, and Kiwi leapt off the chair and ran out of the room.

"Was it something I said?" joked their mum, following Kiwi with her eyes.

Amy and James couldn't stop giggling. If only she knew.

It was a strange day, back at school. Amy thought she did alright in the maths test, but she found it hard to concentrate in her other lessons. She caught herself daydreaming about Cat City and Inspector Furrball, Siam, Paws and Madame Purrfect.

She wondered how Inspector Furrball and Madame Purrfect were doing now that they were back together. A romantic love story with cats! She could just imagine the inspector turning up at her house with a big box of Mrs Ebenry's famous delights and whisking her off to the Catema to see Furrlight.

Amy found herself sniggering in class at such thoughts and each teacher asked her what was so funny. If only she could tell them the story – they would find it so cool. All of the girls and boys would be spellbound at the story. But she couldn't tell. Kiwi would be in serious trouble. "Nothing's funny," she said to the teachers. "Just remembering a TV programme from last night." Nothing funny at all, really.

School seemed less interesting after such an adventure. But, Amy guessed it would only be a matter of time before she could focus fully on everything again and stop thinking about the blue-lit city. One good thing was that her balance had improved – she wasn't nearly as clumsy as she used to be. And she had started noticing the small details in things – the things that never really mattered much before.

For James the day was even stranger. In one class, one of the other boys started laughing at him and James realised he was licking his own hand! Imagine? In class! Spit on his hand?! Ah that has to stop, he thought. In another class he scratched himself behind his ear, over and over again. Dan joked that he had fleas. James realised he really had to focus.

Then there was football practice – even worse. Running for the ball felt weird. For some reason James kept imagining he had four legs and a tail. He kept thinking his tail would hit the other boys running behind him and then, when he realised he was imagining it, someone would tackle him and run off with the ball.

His confused games teacher was staring at him. James was usually one of the best players, but he was running as if he had two left feet. And he kept trying to turn and look at his back while running. When another boy tackled him, James actually hissed! The teacher assumed James hadn't slept well the night before. He made a mental note to have a quiet chat with James sometime soon just to check he was okay.

James went home thinking he was going crazy. He guessed it would take a day or two to adjust to being home again, with just two feet and a tail-less body. Kiwi was going to find this story really funny. James smiled.

Thank you for buying this book.
I hope you enjoyed it.
Please leave a review – feedback is welcome.
Have a kitty nice day.

About the author

Vickie Johnstone lives in London, UK, editing
magazines and writing poetry and prose. Some day
she hopes to live by the sea with fluffy cats and a
lifetime supply of Milky Bar chocolate.

Kiwi's website: *www.kiwiincatcity.com*

Twitter: *@vickiejohnstone*

Blog: *http://vickiejohnstone.blogspot.com*

Goodreads: *http://www.goodreads.com/author/
show/4788773.Vickie_Johnstone*

Printed in Great Britain
by Amazon